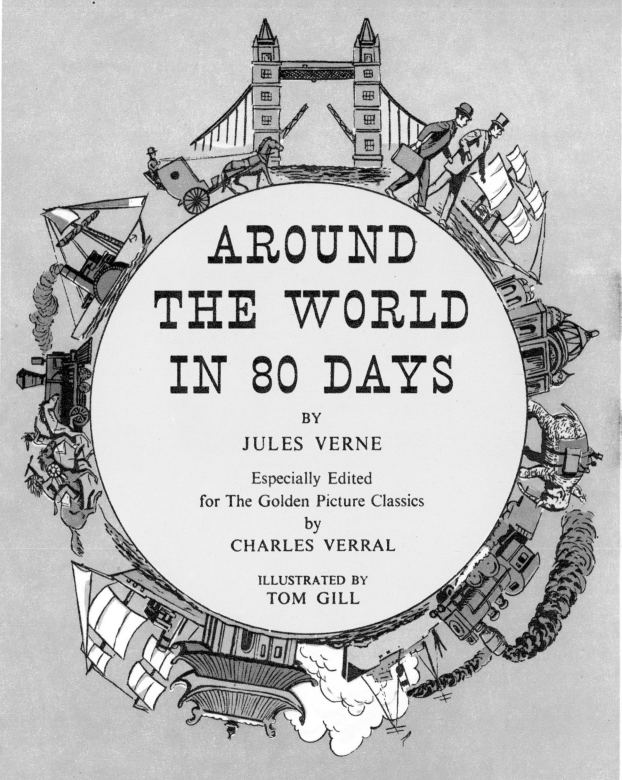

AROUND THE WORLD IN 80 DAYS

BY

JULES VERNE

Especially Edited
for The Golden Picture Classics
by
CHARLES VERRAL

ILLUSTRATED BY
TOM GILL

PURNELL & SONS LIMITED

CONTENTS

The Wager

IT was in the year 1872, when Queen Victoria was Queen, that Mr. Phileas Fogg had his amazing adventure. And it all began because of a wager.

Not that Mr. Fogg was a gambling man. Far from it. His life was run with such clocklike precision that taking a chance on anything was unthinkable.

Phileas Fogg lived alone in a mansion at No. 7, Saville Row, in London. He had one servant to attend to his needs. He demanded little from this man save that he be punctual and exact in all details.

Mr. Fogg's daily habits never varied. In the morning he arose at eight o'clock on the dot. At twenty-three minutes past eight, he was served tea and toast. At thirty-seven minutes past nine, his shaving water was brought to him. At twenty minutes before ten, he began his shaving, washing, and dressing. Then, at half-past eleven he left his house to spend the rest of the day at the exclusive Reform Club to which he belonged.

There he breakfasted and dined each day at the same time, in the same room, at the same table. He seldom took his meals with other club members, and never brought a guest with him. He returned home at the stroke of midnight, to retire at once to bed.

Phileas Fogg was a tall, erect man of some forty years, with fine, handsome features and light hair. His eyes were a clear, startling blue which could go icy cold on occasions. He was so exact that he never took one step too many, always went to his destination by the shortest route, and was never in a hurry.

No one knew much about this calm, deliberate gentleman. That he was undoubtedly rich and had no need to work was obvious. But how he had obtained his money was a mystery. Even the several club members with whom he often played a game of whist knew nothing about his personal affairs.

For years Phileas Fogg maintained his orderly life, doing the same thing at the same time, until one day—on the morning of October 2nd, 1872—an upsetting incident occurred. His servant, James Forster, brought him shaving water heated to 84 degrees Fahrenheit, instead of 86 degrees.

Such a mistake was unforgivable. The luckless Forster was instantly discharged and a new servant sent for.

The new man arrived midway between eleven and half-past eleven. He was a young Frenchman by the name of Jean Passepartout, a pleasant-faced fellow with a good round head and a figure close to being portly. During the brief interview he told Mr. Fogg that he had had many trades. He had been a singer, a circus rider, a gymnast, and a fireman before becoming a valet.

"I have heard that you, Monsieur Phileas Fogg, are the most exact and settled gentleman in England," Passepartout said. "I have therefore come to you in the hope of living a tranquil life."

"Wise indeed," said Mr. Fogg. "You have been well recommended to me. You know my conditions?"

"Yes, monsieur."

"Good! From this moment, you are in my service. What time is it?"

"Twenty-five minutes past eleven," returned Passepartout, drawing an enormous silver watch from his pocket.

"You are slow," said Mr. Fogg.

"Pardon me, monsieur, it is impossible . . ."

"You are four minutes slow. It is now twenty-nine minutes past eleven."

BANK ROBBER EXTRA

Mr. Fogg got up, put his hat on his head, and left the house without another word. As the door closed behind him, he noted that it was half-past eleven. Despite the domestic crisis, the settled course of his life had not been thrown off in the slightest. Nor was it likely to be.

But, for once, Phileas Fogg was wrong, very wrong.

When Mr. Fogg reached the Reform Club in Pall Mall, he had his usual breakfast and then spent several hours reading the newspapers, as was his habit.

The papers were full of accounts of a bank robbery that had occurred three days before. A package of banknotes, worth fifty-five thousand pounds, had been taken from the cashier's table at the Bank of England.

There was a theory that the culprit might not be the usual type of thief. For on the day of the robbery a well-dressed gentleman of polished manners had been observed going to and fro in the paying room where the crime had been committed. A description of the suspect had been obtained and sent to detectives in England and abroad.

It was after Phileas Fogg had eaten his dinner that he heard a group of club members discussing the robbery. He listened attentively. The men were Mr. Fogg's usual partners at whist: Andrew Stuart, an engineer; John Sullivan and Samuel Fallentin, bankers; Thomas Flanagan, a brewer; and Gauthier Ralph, one of the directors of the Bank of England.

"The bank will never recover the money," said Stuart.

"On the contrary," broke in Ralph, "I feel confident that we will put our hands on the robber. Skilful detectives have been sent to all the principal ports of America and the Continent. And a reward has been offered of two thousand pounds, together with five per cent of the sum recovered. He'll be a clever fellow if he escapes capture."

"I maintain the chances are in favour of the thief," said Stuart.

"Where can he go?" asked Ralph. "No country is safe for him."

"Oh, I don't know. The world is big enough."

"It was once," said Phileas Fogg. abruptly breaking into the conversation.

Stuart turned toward him. "What do you mean by 'once,' Mr. Fogg? Has the world grown smaller?"

"Certainly," returned Phileas Fogg.

"I agree with Mr. Fogg," said Ralph. "The world *has* grown smaller, since a man can now go round it ten times more quickly than a hundred years ago. That's why the search for this thief will be more likely to succeed."

"Not at all," said Stuart. "Just because you can go round the world in three months . . ."

"In eighty days," interrupted Phileas Fogg. "Here is the estimate made by the *Daily Telegraph*." He indicated a section in the paper.

From London to Suez via Mont Cenis and Brindisi, by rail and steamboats	7	days
From Suez to Bombay, by steamer	13	"
From Bombay to Calcutta, by rail	3	"
From Calcutta to Hong Kong, by steamer	13	"
From Hong Kong to Yokohama, by steamer	6	"
From Yokohama to San Francisco, by steamer	22	"
From San Francisco to New York, by rail	7	"
From New York to London, by steamer and rail	9	"
TOTAL	**80 days**	

"But that doesn't take into account bad weather, contrary winds, ship-wrecks, railway accidents, and so on," exclaimed Stuart.

"All included," returned Phileas Fogg.

"But suppose the Hindus or Indians pull up the rails. Suppose they stop the trains and scalp the passengers."

"All included," calmly retorted Mr. Fogg.

"You are right, theoretically, Mr. Fogg," said Stuart. "But practically . . ."

"Practically, also, Mr. Stuart."

Mr. Stuart was becoming irritated. "I'd like to see you do it in eighty days. I would wager four thousand pounds that such a journey, made under these conditions, is impossible."

"On the contrary, it's quite possible," returned Mr. Fogg.

Mr. Stuart was now quite excited. "Well, make it, then!" he challenged.

"I should like nothing better."

"When?"

"At once. Only I warn you that I shall do it at your expense."

Stuart ran a feverish hand across his brow. "Very well, Mr. Fogg," said he. "I'll wager the four thousand."

"Calm yourself, my dear Stuart," said Fallentin. "It's only a joke."

"When I say I'll wager," returned Stuart, "I mean it."

"All right," said Mr. Fogg. He turned to the others. "I have twenty thousand pounds on deposit at my bank which I will willingly risk."

"Twenty thousand pounds!" cried Sullivan. "Twenty thousand pounds which you would lose by a single acci-dental delay!"

9

"The unforeseen does not exist," quietly replied Mr. Fogg. "To repeat, I will wager twenty thousand pounds that I will be able to make the tour of the world in eighty days or less; in nineteen hundred and twenty hours, or a hundred and fifteen thousand, two hundred minutes. Would each of you five gentlemen wish to wager four thousand against my twenty thousand?"

Messrs. Stuart, Fallentin, Sullivan, Flanagan, and Ralph withdrew and held a brief conference.

"We accept," they announced presently.

"Excellent," said Mr. Fogg. "The train leaves for Dover at a quarter before nine. I will take it."

"This very evening?" asked Stuart.

"This very evening," returned Phileas Fogg. "Today is Wednesday, the 2nd of October. I shall be due in London, in this very room of the Reform Club, on Saturday, the 21st of December, at a quarter before nine P.M.; otherwise the twenty thousand pounds now deposited in my name will belong to you gentlemen. Here is a check for the amount."

Phileas Fogg left the Reform Club at twenty-five minutes past seven and proceeded to his home. Passepartout was more than surprised to see his master.

"But it is not midnight," said Passepartout, showing his watch.

"I know it," Mr. Fogg said. "I don't blame you for being upset. Now give me your attention. We start for Dover and Calais in ten minutes. We are going around the world."

Passepartout seemed about to collapse. "Around the world!"

"In eighty days," responded Mr. Fogg. "We haven't a moment to lose. We will take no trunks, only a carpet-bag with a few shirts, socks, and toilet articles for me and the same for you. We'll buy our clothes on the way. Bring my mackintosh and travelling cloak and some stout shoes, though we shall do little walking. Make haste!"

Still stunned by Mr. Fogg's decision, Passepartout left to make preparations for the trip. Why would so domestic a person as Phileas Fogg make a sudden departure like this? Around the world in eighty days! Was his master a fool? Or was this a joke? Passepartout shook his head in bewilderment.

Meanwhile Mr. Fogg had gone to his safe in an upper room. From the safe he removed a roll of banknotes amounting to twenty thousand pounds. The twenty thousand was half his fortune. The other half, which was deposited in his bank, he had wagered. Yet, in order to win the wager, he reasoned he would have to spend considerable money for the trip, perhaps the full amount.

Presently, equipped with his passport and a guidebook showing the arrival and departure of steamers and railways, Mr. Fogg joined Passepartout, who had packed the carpetbag, and slipped the roll of banknotes inside.

"Take good care of this bag. There are twenty thousand pounds in it," Mr. Fogg said to the startled Passepartout. "Now let us depart."

Securely locking the front door after them, Phileas Fogg and Passepartout took a cab to the Charing Cross railway station, arriving at twenty minutes past eight. Two first-class tickets for Paris were quickly purchased. Then as Mr. Fogg and his valet were crossing the station to the train, Phileas Fogg saw his five friends from the Reform Club.

"Well, gentlemen," said he, "I'm off, you see. If you will examine my passport when I get back, you will be able to judge whether I have accomplished the journey agreed upon."

"Quite unnecessary, Mr. Fogg," said Ralph politely. "We will trust your word as a gentleman of honour."

"In eighty days I am due in London again," said Phileas Fogg. "On Saturday, the 21st of December, 1872, at a quarter before nine P.M. Good-bye, gentlemen."

Phileas Fogg and his servant seated themselves in a first-class carriage at twenty minutes before nine. Five minutes later the whistle screamed and the train to Dover slowly glided out of the station.

The race around the world had begun.

Suspicion at Suez

FOR the first few days all went well. The two travellers reached Paris early Thursday morning and took the train for Turin, Italy. At Turin, they headed south to the Italian port of Brindisi, arriving on Saturday afternoon, October 5th. There, Mr. Fogg and Passepartout boarded the steamship *Mongolia*, which promptly set sail, bound for Bombay, India, via the Suez Canal.

Four days later, after crossing the Mediterranean Sea and passing through the great canal, the *Mongolia* dropped anchor in the port of Suez at the head of the Red Sea. The stop was to be brief, just long enough for a fresh supply of coal to be loaded on the ship. Then the *Mongolia* would be on her way again. But, during the coaling, passengers could go ashore if they wished to inspect the town of Suez.

Phileas Fogg had no interest in seeing the town. As for the few errands that had to be done in Suez, Passepartout could look after them.

Mr. Fogg remained in his cabin and opened the carpetbag. From it he took a notebook in which he had made careful entries of the time and arrival at each principal point along the route. And in neat precise writing he brought the record up to date. So far, the journey had taken just what he had estimated— a total of 158½ hours; or six and a half days. They had neither gained nor lost an hour. They were exactly on schedule.

But, even at that moment, trouble was brewing for the exacting Mr. Fogg. On the dock at Suez, some distance from where the *Mongolia* lay anchored, a small, slightly built man by the name of Fix was pacing up and down. Fix was a detective, dispatched from England in search of the bank robber.

It was his task to inspect each passenger who came ashore at Suez and to follow all who seemed suspicious or who bore a resemblance to the description of the well-dressed gentleman who was suspected of committing the crime. The description had arrived two days before from the police headquarters in London. It now lay in an inner pocket, but Fix had no need to refer to it. He had committed the words to memory. Indeed, he felt positive that he would be able to recognize the suspect instantly. And a sixth sense told him that the man was aboard the *Mongolia*. He hoped so. He could certainly use the reward.

Boats were now proceeding from the steamship toward the dock, crowded with passengers who were coming ashore.

Fix took up a position close to where the boats would unload. It seemed natural to suppose that if the robber had travelled on the *Mongolia* he would land at Suez and flee to the Dutch or French colonies rather than go to India. For in India, being English soil, he would be in constant danger of arrest.

As the passengers from the *Mongolia* arrived at the pier, Fix eagerly scanned each face. But not one resembled the description of the suspected criminal.

Shaken with disappointment, Fix was about to turn away when one of the passengers came up to him. It was Passepartout.

"Could you point out the English consulate to me, monsieur?" Passepartout asked. "I wish to get this passport visaed." He held out the document.

The detective took the passport and with a rapid glance read the description of its owner. A start of surprise nearly escaped him, for the description in the passport was identical with that of the bank robber.

"Is this your passport?" Fix asked Passepartout.

"No, it's my master's. He stayed on board."

Fix thought quickly. "But he must go to the consulate in person to establish his identity."

"Is that necessary?"

"Quite," said Fix. A flush of excitement showed in his cheeks.

"And where is the consulate?" asked Passepartout.

"There, on the corner of the square," said Fix, pointing to a house two hundred steps off.

"Very well," said Passepartout. "I'll go and fetch my master. He won't like being disturbed, I can tell you."

The moment Passepartout turned to go back to the steamer, Fix started for the consul's office. After a short delay, he was admitted.

"Consul," said he, "I have strong reason to believe that the rogue who stole those fifty-five thousand pounds from the Bank of England is a passenger on the *Mongolia*. He is coming here to have his passport visaed. I hope you will refuse to do so."

"Why?" the consul asked. "If the passport is genuine I have no right to refuse."

"Don't you understand, sir?" the detective said. "I must somehow keep this man here in Suez until I can get a warrant from London for his arrest."

"That is your lookout," the consul said. "I cannot . . ."

The consul did not finish his sentence, for as he spoke there was a knock on the door and Mr. Fogg and Passepartout entered.

Fix retired to a dark corner of the room where he remained staring at Phileas Fogg.

"You are Mr. Phileas Fogg?" said the consul, after reading the passport that had been handed him.

"I am. And this is my servant, a Frenchman, named Passepartout."

"You are from London?"

"Yes."

"And you are going . . ."

"To Bombay. I wish to have my passport visaed to prove I came by Suez."

"Very good, sir," said the consul. He proceeded to sign and date the passport, then added his official seal.

Mr. Fogg paid the customary fee, bowed stiffly, and went out, followed by Passepartout.

"Well?" queried Fix.

"He looks and acts like a perfectly honest man," replied the consul.

"Read this description of the suspected thief, sir," the detective said, putting the paper down in front of the consul.

When that official had done so, Fix continued, "Do you not think that Phileas Fogg resembles, feature by feature, this man?"

"I concede that," said the consul. "But you know, all descriptions . . ."

"I'll make certain of it," interrupted Fix. "The servant is a Frenchman and can't help talking. I'll pump him."

And the detective hurried off in search of Passepartout. Much to Fix's delight, he had little trouble finding the Frenchman. Passepartout was on the dock alone, Mr. Fogg having returned to the ship.

"Well, my friend," Fix said easily, "now that your passport is visaed you are looking over the town?"

"Yes," Passepartout said. "We've been travelling so fast that I've had little chance to see anything."

"You are in a great hurry, then?"

"I am not, but my master is. By the way, I have been instructed to buy some shoes and shirts. We came away without trunks, only a carpetbag."

"You left London hastily then?"

"Rather. Last Friday at eight o'clock in the evening, Monsieur Fogg came home from his club and three-quarters of an hour afterward we were off."

"But where is your master going?"

"Round the world. In eighty days. He says it's a wager, but, between us, I don't believe a word of it. There's something else in the wind."

"Ah!" murmured Fix. "Mr. Fogg must be a rich man to be making such a trip."

"Rich, indeed! He is carrying an enormous sum in brand-new banknotes with him. And he doesn't spare the money on the way, either. He has offered a large reward to the engineer of the *Mongolia* if he gets us to Bombay ahead of time."

"You have known your master a long time?"

"No, indeed. I entered his service the very day we left London."

The detective was breathing rapidly now as his excitement mounted. The hasty departure from London soon after the robbery; the large sum of money carried; the eagerness to reach distant countries; the story of a foolhardy bet; all confirmed Fix's theory that Mr. Phileas Fogg was his man.

"Come," he said to Passepartout, "I will show you an excellent shop where you may buy what you want."

"You are most kind, monsieur," Passepartout said. "But don't let me lose the steamer."

"You have plenty of time," Fix said as they walked along. "It's only twelve o'clock."

Passepartout pulled out his big watch. "Twelve!" he exclaimed. "Why, it's only eight minutes before ten."

"Your watch is slow."

"*My* watch!" exclaimed Passepartout indignantly. "I'll have you know, monsieur, that this timepiece has come down from my great-grandfather. It does not vary five minutes in the year."

"I have it," Fix said. "You have kept London time, which is two hours behind that of Suez. You ought to regulate your watch at noon in each country."

"I regulate my watch? Never!"

"Well, then, it will not agree with the sun."

"So much the worse for the sun, monsieur."

Fix was paying little attention to what Passepartout said, for a plan of action was beginning to form in his mind. He pointed ahead.

"There is the shop where you may make your purchases," he said. "Now I must leave you."

After Passepartout had thanked him politely again, the detective hurried away. He went immediately to the telegraph office and sent off a dispatch to Scotland Yard.

SUEZ TO LONDON
ROWAN, COMMISSIONER OF POLICE, SCOTLAND YARD:

I HAVE FOUND THE BANK ROBBER, PHILEAS FOGG. SEND WITHOUT DELAY WARRANT OF ARREST TO BOMBAY.

FIX, DETECTIVE

The Sights of Bombay

FOR almost a full week, the name of Phileas Fogg had been on everyone's lips in England. Scarcely had he and Passepartout left London than news of the bet had spread rapidly through the Reform Club and from the club it had got into the papers. The "tour of the world" was disputed and argued. Some took sides with Phileas Fogg. Others declared that it was utterly impossible to go round the world in eighty days.

The Times, Standard, Morning Post, and *Daily News,* and twenty other highly respectable newspapers throughout England, called Mr. Fogg's project sheer madness. The *Daily Telegraph* alone supported him. Many people thought him a lunatic.

The Royal Geographical Society issued a bulletin pointing out the utter folly of such an undertaking. It stressed that everything would be against the travellers. Mr. Fogg might be able to rely on trains arriving on time in Europe where distances were moderate. But he certainly could not count on crossing India in three days and the United States in seven. There were breakdowns of machinery to be considered, accidents, bad weather. Would he not find himself at the mercy of winds and fogs when travelling by ship in winter? Was it uncommon for the best ocean steamers to be two or three days behind schedule? One single delay or one missed connection could defeat him.

But in spite of all this, interest in Mr. Fogg and his race round the world mounted steadily. Heavy wagers were made for or against him not only by members of the Reform Club but by the public as well.

19

It was into this atmosphere that the detective Fix's dispatch from Suez came. The effect was sensational.

Phileas Fogg was suddenly no longer the polished gentleman engaged in a colourful adventure, but a bank robber. His photograph, which hung with those of the rest of the members at the Reform Club, was carefully examined. All agreed that it tallied, feature by feature, with the description of the robber.

The mysterious habits of Phileas Fogg were recalled: his solitary ways, his abrupt departure. And it now seemed clear that he had made the outrageous wager as a trick to throw the police off his trail.

Meanwhile, her coaling completed, the good ship *Mongolia* had left Suez and was proceeding under full steam for Aden, at the south end of the Red Sea. Aboard her rode the deliberate Mr. Fogg, quite unaware of the commotion that had been stirred up in England. Nor was he aware that, just before the anchor had been lifted, an extra passenger, carrying a small bag, had rushed aboard in the person of Fix.

The voyage across thirteen hundred and ten watery miles between Suez and Aden was far from placid. Violent storms churned the Red Sea into a fury and caused the ship to pitch and roll.

Phileas Fogg gave no sign that he was concerned. He ate four meals a day and spent the rest of his waking hours quietly playing whist with three fellow passengers.

As for Passepartout, he was rather enjoying the voyage, being well fed and lodged. Not so Fix, the detective. He was in a miserable state. The rolling motion of the ship had had its effect on his stomach. Furthermore, he was tense with anxiety over the best way to lay hands on the bank robber, Phileas Fogg.

True enough, Scotland Yard would undoubtedly send the warrant of arrest by the fastest mail to Bombay, as requested. But that would take well over two weeks. What if this rogue, Fogg, failed to loiter in Bombay? What if he should continue on his pretended tour of the world?

Fix held his head in his hands. Somehow, he would have to find out what Phileas Fogg's plans were. And the only chance seemed to lie in making contact with his talkative servant.

So one clear day when the *Mongolia* was, for once, travelling on an even keel, Fix saw to it that he ran into Passepartout on deck.

Passepartout recognized him with a cry of delight.

"Are you not the gentleman who so kindly volunteered to guide me at Suez?" he asked.

Fix bowed. "The same. Fix is my name. How nice to see you again."

"The pleasure is mine," said Passepartout, politely returning the bow. "Where are you bound, Monsieur Fix?"

"Like you for Bombay," said Fix. Then he added carelessly, "Such a beautiful city, Bombay. So much to see. Mosques, minarets, temples, fakirs, pagodas, snakes, elephants. I trust you and your master intend to spend some time there."

"I would like nothing better," said Passepartout earnestly. "But Mr. Fogg still pretends that he is making a tour of the world and he seems inclined to go right on."

"Perhaps you might convince him of the scenic beauties he will miss," said Fix, desperately.

"I shall indeed try, Monsieur Fix."

After this meeting, the detective got into the habit of chatting with Passepartout at every opportunity. But the tidings the Frenchman brought regarding a possible stay in Bombay were discouraging. Mr. Fogg apparently was set on pressing forward.

Any hope that Fix had that the *Mongolia* might be delayed by bad weather or some mechanical breakdown was dashed. Spurred on by Mr. Fogg's promised reward, the ship's engineer pushed the vessel at such a speed that she arrived at Aden on October 14th, fifteen hours ahead of schedule.

Mr. Fogg and Passepartout went ashore to have the passport visaed. Fix followed, taking care he was not observed. There was always the chance that the bank robber might use this opportunity to disappear.

But Mr. Fogg returned on board to resume his whist playing. Shortly thereafter, with her coaling finished, the *Mongolia* once more set forth. Next stop—Bombay.

There was nothing for the detective to do but trust that Phileas Fogg would, for some reason, remain long enough in Bombay for the warrant to show up. But during the voyage across the Indian Ocean, Fix's tension mounted with every thrust of the ship's propeller.

On Sunday, October 20th, toward noon, the Indian coast was sighted. At half-past four, the *Mongolia* came alongside the dock at Bombay, a full two days ahead of time.

Mr. Fogg opened his carpetbag and paid the engineer the promised reward. Then, he calmly entered the gain of the two days in his notebook.

After bidding good-bye to his whist partners, Phileas Fogg and Passepartout descended the gangway to the shore. Close behind them, mingling with the crowd, came Fix, his face a mask of concern. What was the bank robber going to do?

The detective soon got the answer. Concealed behind some packing boxes on the dock, he heard Phileas Fogg tell Passepartout to purchase additional shirts and shoes.

"Meet me at the railway station at half-past seven," said Mr. Fogg. "The train for Calcutta leaves at exactly eight this evening."

"We are not staying to see the sights of Bombay?" asked Passepartout.

"Certainly not," replied Mr. Fogg. "Make sure that you are at the station in plenty of time."

Momentarily dazed by the news, Fix watched Mr. Fogg and his servant go their separate ways, Passepartout to shop, Phileas Fogg to the passport office. The robber was clearing out of Bombay that very day. How on earth could he be restrained?

There seemed to be only one chance and Fix pursued it. He hurried to the headquarters of the Bombay police. Making himself known as a London detective, he was taken to the director, to whom he hastily explained the facts of the case.

"Since the document from London has not yet arrived," said Fix, "will *you* issue a warrant of arrest for this criminal? Otherwise he will be gone."

The director shook his head. "No. This matter concerns the London office," said he. "They alone can legally deliver the warrant. It would be a different matter if the crime had been committed on Indian soil."

A light began to glow in Fix's sunken eyes. What if he could get the rogue, Fogg, or his servant to break a law while in Bombay? Wouldn't that do the trick?

But the surge of hope died as quickly as it had been born. A criminal such as this one would be most careful not to do anything to attract police attention. All he could do, Fix decided, was to leave instructions to forward the warrant of arrest to Calcutta while he, himself, followed his quarry in person. He could not afford to lose track of Fogg.

23

So thinking, the detective left police headquarters and directed his steps toward the station to await the coming of Phileas Fogg.

While Fix was absorbed in his problem, Passepartout had gone about his shopping, his heart heavy. He was sorely disappointed that he would be unable to see any of the magnificent sights in Bombay which his good friend, Monsieur Fix, had so vividly described.

After purchasing the necessary shirts and shoes, Passepartout discovered that he had considerable time to spend before he was to meet his master at the station. He therefore took a leisurely walk, eying with interest the people of many nationalities who thronged the streets. There were Persians with pointed caps, Banyas with round turbans, Parsees with black mitres, and long-robed Armenians.

It happened to be the day of a Parsee festival and there was a religious carnival being held with processions and gaiety. Indian dancing girls cavorted airily to the sound of viols and the clanging of tambourines.

Passepartout watched with staring eyes and gaping mouth until the procession had passed. Then, as he was making his way toward the railway station, he happened to notice the splendid pagoda on Malabar Hill. He became seized with a desire to see its interior.

The Frenchman did not know that it was forbidden for a Christian to enter certain Indian temples, and that even the faithful must not go in without removing their shoes at the door. Nor had Passepartout any idea that the British government dealt out severe punishments to anyone disregarding the practices of the native religions.

So, intending no harm, Passepartout entered the pagoda. Inside, he was lost in admiration of the splendid decorations when suddenly he found himself set upon by three enraged priests and flung to the floor. Before the dazed Passepartout could defend himself, his attackers tore off his shoes and began to beat him, shouting wildly.

The agile Frenchman was soon on his feet and lost little time in knocking down two of his long-gowned attackers. Then he rushed out of the pagoda as fast as his legs could carry him.

In the meantime, the detective, Fix, had arrived at the railway station, as had Phileas Fogg. By remaining out of sight behind a pillar, Fix had kept Mr. Fogg under constant observation. His intention was to board the same train to Calcutta as the bank robber.

It was five minutes before eight when Passepartout, hatless and shoeless, sprinted breathless into the station.

He had also lost his parcel of shirts and shoes in the scuffle.

Choking and gasping, Passepartout told Mr. Fogg of the appalling thing that had happened.

"This could have been serious," said Phileas Fogg coldly. "I trust it will not occur again."

With that, Mr. Fogg stalked off to board the train with Passepartout meekly following.

From his place of concealment, Fix had heard every word Passepartout had uttered and a flush of excitement was reddening his face.

"Ah," he breathed, "a serious crime has been committed on Indian soil. Now I can get a warrant for arrest. They will fall into the hands of the police when they arrive in Calcutta."

Satisfied, Fix allowed the train to Calcutta to leave without him and hastily started back to the Bombay police station.

"I've got my man," he rejoiced. "I've really got him now."

Sacrifice at Dawn

On the train, Passepartout and Phileas Fogg were surprised to find themselves seated opposite Brigadier-General Sir Francis Cromarty who had been one of Mr. Fogg's whist partners on the *Mongolia*. Sir Francis was on his way to Benares to join his brigade.

From time to time, as the train rushed through the night, Phileas Fogg and the brigadier exchanged a few words. But it was clear that Sir Francis thought any person who would race madly around the world because of a wager was decidedly odd.

Not so Passepartout. Up until their arrival in Bombay, he had hoped that their journey would end there. Now that they were hurrying on, he was beginning to believe his master's story. And a feeling of tense excitement was taking hold of him. What a bold venture this was. How daring! But would they make it in the specified time?

All that night and into the next day the train rattled on, past jungles inhabited by tigers and other wild beasts, through dense forests where huge elephants could be seen.

At noon, on October 21, a brief stop was made at Burhampoor where the passengers ate a hasty breakfast. There Passepartout managed to buy some Indian slippers into which he gratefully slid his stocking feet. Then the passengers climbed aboard again and the train sped on its way.

27

At eight o'clock the following morning, October 22, the train came to an abrupt halt near a small village and the conductor announced, "All passengers will get out here!"

"What do you mean?" asked Sir Francis.

"Just what I say," replied the conductor. "This is as far as the train goes. The railway isn't finished. There's still a matter of fifty miles of track to be laid from here to Allahabad where the line begins again."

"But you sell tickets from Bombay to Calcutta," Sir Francis spluttered. "The newspapers announced the line was completed."

"Then the newspapers were wrong," said the conductor. "Passengers must provide their own transportation from this village to Allahabad."

Passepartout doubled up his fists. He would willingly have knocked the conductor down. What an outrage!

But Phileas Fogg remained perfectly at ease.

"Do not be upset," he said calmly. "I knew some obstacles would sooner or later arise and I have made allowances. I have two days, which I have gained, to sacrifice. A steamer leaves Calcutta for Hong Kong at noon on the 25th. This is the 22nd. We shall reach Calcutta in time. Now we must look about for some means of transportation to Allahabad."

Most of the passengers had apparently known about the missing section of track. And by the time Mr. Fogg, Passepartout, and Sir Francis left the train, every available carriage, wagon, and pony had been hired.

"We shall go afoot then," said the dauntless Phileas Fogg.

Passepartout gazed at his frail Indian slippers and winced.

"Wait, monsieur," said he. "Perhaps I can find something."

He returned in triumph a short while later. "I have come upon an elephant," said he.

The elephant belonged to an Indian who stubbornly refused to rent the beast. Quite undisturbed, Mr. Fogg proceeded to offer to buy it outright. Nor did he seem bothered one whit when the Indian held out for the staggering sum of two thousand pounds.

Passepartout gazed appalled at his master as Mr. Fogg opened the carpetbag and casually counted out the bank notes. What a price! And what in heaven's name would Mr. Fogg do with the elephant after they reached Allahabad? Would he take the beast with them on the rest of the journey?

A young Parsee who spoke excellent English was soon found to act as guide and driver. A saddle cloth was thrown across the elephant's back. Two uncomfortable howdahs, one on either side, were attached to the beast's flanks. Then, with Phileas Fogg in one howdah, Sir Francis in the other, Passepartout astride the saddle cloth, and the Parsee perched on the elephant's neck, the expedition started.

It had been impressed on the driver that all possible speed should be shown, so the Parsee headed the animal through a forest of palms at a brisk trot. The lumbering gait had a violent effect on the passengers. Mr. Fogg and Sir Francis were jostled unmercifully in the howdahs. Poor Passepartout bounced like a clown on a springboard until he thought every tooth in his head would be loosened.

At noon they stopped for a much-needed rest and for something to eat, but were soon on their way again. The course taken by the Parsee led through wild and mysterious country. From time to time they sighted bands of ferocious Indians who made angry and threatening gestures at them. Monkeys scurried from their path and the growls of panthers could be heard.

They had covered almost half the fifty miles to Allahabad when they reached a deserted hut where they spent the night. Promptly at six the next morning, the journey was resumed.

"We shall undoubtedly reach Allahabad this evening," said Sir Francis.

But at four o'clock that afternoon, just when it seemed that the trip would be successfully accomplished, the Parsee suddenly guided the elephant behind a thicket and jumped to the ground.

"What is it?" asked Sir Francis.

The Parsee gestured for silence and slipped away through the trees. In a few moments he was back.

"A procession of Brahmins is coming this way," he said. "It might be dangerous if they see us."

Presently the sound of a droning song, accompanied by the din of brass instruments, was heard. From their place of concealment behind the leaves of the thicket, Phileas Fogg and Passepartout and Sir Francis saw a strange procession pass. In front were priests and a crowd of men, women, and children. Behind them came a cart, drawn by zebus, on which rested a hideous statue with four arms.

"The goddess Kali," whispered Sir Francis. "The goddess of love and death."

Directly behind the cart came a group of Brahmins leading a young and very beautiful woman. She was ornately gowned and wore much jewellery. She seemed in a daze and stumbled and faltered as she walked.

Following her were a number of sturdy men, armed with sabres and pistols, who carried a hammock-like litter suspended from poles. Laid out in the hammock was the body of an old man. He had a jewelled turban on his head and was garbed in the magnificent raiment of a rajah.

Bringing up the rear were many musicians and fakirs who danced about and uttered loud cries.

"It is a suttee," said Sir Francis after the procession had gone by.

"What's that?" asked Passepartout.

"A human sacrifice," the brigadier explained. "The woman you just saw is the wife of the dead man. She will be burned alive when her husband's body is consumed by flames at dawn."

"The scoundrels!" cried Passepartout

"It is a barbarous native custom which the English are trying to stop," said Sir Francis. "But it is difficult to suppress in these outlying districts. In most cases, the wife wishes to sacrifice herself so that she can join her husband in the beyond."

"This time it is *not* a voluntary sacrifice," said the Parsee.

"Why doesn't the poor woman try to escape?" asked Passepartout.

"They have her drugged with fumes of hemp and opium so that she cannot resist," said the guide. "She is being taken to the pagoda of Pillaji, two miles from here, where she will pass the night. At the first light of dawn the sacrifice will take place."

"You seem to know a good deal about this affair," said Sir Francis.

"Yes, officer, I do," replied the Parsee. He went on to give an account of the victim. Her name was Aouda and she was a celebrated beauty of the Parsee race, the daughter of a rich Bombay merchant. She had been given an English education and was very intelligent. Left an orphan, she had been married against her will to a wealthy rajah and had already tried to escape from the horrible fate that was awaiting her.

"But she was caught," the guide concluded. "And now she is helpless."

Phileas Fogg listened to the recital without a change of expression. But when the guide again mounted the elephant and was about to urge it on its way, Mr. Fogg stopped him.

"Suppose we save this woman," said he, turning to Sir Francis.

"Save her!" exclaimed Sir Francis. "My dear sir, are you serious?"

"Of course I'm serious," said Mr. Fogg. "I have twelve hours to spare. I can devote them to that."

Sir Francis stared at Phileas Fogg, thunderstruck. "You had seemed to me a person without feeling," said he. "But you are a man of heart!"

"Sometimes," replied Phileas Fogg, quietly, "when I have the time."

The project held an immense appeal for Passepartout. To think that his master would risk the success of his tour, not to speak of his life and liberty, to save a beautiful young woman, stirred the Frenchman deeply. Under that icy English exterior, he realized, dwelt indeed a pulsing heart and a soul.

Sir Francis, too, was in full support of the scheme. Even the guide fell in with the idea.

"I am a Parsee and this woman is a Parsee," said he. "Command me as you will. But let me give this warning. If we are captured, we will experience horrible tortures and death."

"That is foreseen," replied Mr. Fogg, idly dusting off his hands with a handkerchief. "I think we should wait until night before acting. But first we shall go to the vicinity of the pagoda where the young woman is to be imprisoned. . . . Proceed, my good man."

Half an hour later, the elephant was brought to a stop in a wooded glade near the pagoda of Pillaji. There the party waited.

When night had fallen, Mr. Fogg gave the signal and the men moved forward under cover of the trees until the minarets of the pagoda loomed up ahead. In a clearing a short distance from the pagoda stood a stack of wooden logs, on the top of which lay the body of the rajah.

"The funeral pyre," muttered Sir Francis.

Passepartout shivered at the sight. At dawn the fair young woman would be brought forth and placed on that dreadful pile of wood beside the body of her husband. Then the logs would be set ablaze to consume the dead and the living. Passepartout ground his teeth in his agitation.

Scattered across the ground were groups of Indians. They were stretched out in a drunken sleep caused by liquid opium and hemp. But to the disappointment of all, armed guards were stationed at the doors of the pagoda. They paced back and forth, their naked sabres glinting in the light from many torches.

"It will be impossible to force an entrance there," said Phileas Fogg. "But perhaps the guards will also go to sleep. We shall see."

The four men crouched down, watching. Time passed and there was no sign of any relaxation on the part of the guards.

At midnight, Mr. Fogg said, "Let us try from the rear. We may gain an entrance there."

The party cautiously circled the pagoda and approached it from behind. Passepartout's heart leaped. The way seemed clear; no guards were to be seen. But his hope vanished abruptly when he saw that there was no door or entrance in the rear wall.

"We can never get in this way," said Passepartout. "There is no opening."

"Then we shall have to make one," said Phileas Fogg. "Get out your pocketknives."

Stealthily the pagoda was approached until the four men were crouched against the base of the wall. Under Mr. Fogg's whispered directions Passepartout and the Parsee got busy with pocketknives.

The temple wall was, happily, built of brick and wood which could be penetrated with little difficulty. Working quietly, Passepartout and the guide loosened several bricks and drew them out. They had made an opening two feet wide when, suddenly, a cry came from inside the pagoda.

"We have been discovered," said Phileas Fogg in his matter-of-fact voice. "We must retreat."

The return to the cover of the woods was promptly executed. They had no sooner flattened themselves on the ground when a number of the rajah's guards appeared around the side of the temple, carrying torches. The guards made no effort to search for the intruders, but a group of them remained at the rear of the pagoda, obviously to repel any further attempt.

"We have failed," said Sir Francis. "We have no choice but to go away."

"Not at all," said Phileas Fogg. "A chance to rescue the young woman may present itself at the last moment. I am not due at Allahabad tomorrow until noon. I can afford to risk a few more hours."

Little could be gained by remaining at the rear of the pagoda, so the party returned to the front where they could stay hidden by the trees and observe the funeral pyre and the forms of the sleeping natives.

Passepartout kept himself a little apart from the others, excitedly going over an idea that had struck him like a flash. Then, without a word to his companions, the Frenchman slipped away through the darkness.

35

Mr. Fogg sat on the ground, his eyes fixed on the scene before him. He spoke neither to the Parsee nor to Sir Francis. They, too, remained utterly still. Hours passed and the sky began to lighten.

The slumbering multitude gradually awoke. Songs and cries and the sound of tambourines could be heard. The hour of the sacrifice was at hand.

Abruptly the doors of the pagoda swung open and, in the light from inside, Phileas Fogg spied the young woman. For a moment she seemed to have shaken off her drugged stupor and was trying to escape from her executioner. But it was no use. She was led forward toward the funeral pyre. The cries of the crowd grew louder and wilder as the people surged around the place of sacrifice.

Mr. Fogg was now on his feet and Sir Francis noticed that he had a knife clutched in his hand.

At the base of the wooden logs, the young woman collapsed in a swoon. Her limp form was lifted to the top of the funeral pyre and stretched out beside the body of the rajah. A torch was brought and the wood, heavily soaked with oil, instantly took fire. A great cloud of heavy smoke billowed up.

At that moment, Phileas Fogg surged forward. Only the grip of Sir Francis and the Parsee restrained him. Quickly, he shook them off.

But before Mr. Fogg could launch himself into action again, a wild shriek of terror arose from the multitude. They threw themselves flat on the ground.

For there, on the funeral pyre, in the midst of the swirling curtain of smoke, the figure of a man wearing a turban had suddenly arisen. The man lifted the unconscious young woman in his arms and leaped to the ground.

A shout went up. "The rajah returns to life!"

Fakirs and guards and holy men lay terrified, their faces on the ground, not daring to lift their eyes and behold such a miracle. Even Mr. Fogg came close to exhibiting astonishment.

The man in the turban, supporting the limp body of the young woman, strode rapidly through the terrified crowd. He came straight to the trees where Mr. Fogg, Sir Francis, and the Parsee stood in stunned surprise.

When he was quite close, the man said, "Let us be off!"

Only then did Phileas Fogg and the others realize that the turbaned man was Passepartout.

There was no time for questions. Breaking into a run, the entire party raced for the glade where the elephant had been left. Speedily, they mounted the giant beast.

They were not a moment too soon. Shouts of rage came from behind, telling them that the real rajah's body had been discovered. The enraged guards fired a volley of bullets through the woods. But by that time, the Parsee had urged the elephant to full speed and the pursuers were soon outdistanced.

Arrest in Calcutta

"My dear fellow," exclaimed Sir Francis to Passepartout, "how did you do it?"

Now that the rash rescue had been accomplished, Passepartout had a desire to laugh. Between chuckles, he explained how he had stolen through the darkness and stationed himself behind the funeral pyre. When the wood had been set alight and the great cloud of smoke had arisen, he had nimbly climbed to the top of the stack, snatched the turban from the dead rajah, and slapped it on his own head. In the half-light of dawn and with smoke billowing thickly around him, his features had been masked from the crowd. They had assumed from the turban that he was indeed the rajah returned to life.

"It was easy after that," said Passepartout. "All I did was lift up the young woman, jump to the ground, and run." His body shook with laughter. "To think that I, the ex-gymnast, ex-fireman, ex-circus rider should have been, for a

few moments, an Indian rajah and the husband of a charming woman."

Phileas Fogg was silent during the recital. But the one approving nod he gave in Passepartout's direction was enough thanks for the Frenchman.

As for the young Indian woman, Aouda, she had remained unconscious throughout and was now wrapped in a travelling blanket in one of the howdahs.

Sir Francis, who was familiar with the effects produced by the fumes of hemp, assured Mr. Fogg that she would recover her senses but not for some time. He strongly advised that Aouda be removed from India. Otherwise she would be searched for and done to death by the rajah's family.

Thanks to the skilful guidance of the Parsee, the elephant rapidly covered the remaining distance to the holy city of Allahabad at the junction of the Ganges and Jumna Rivers. It was ten o'clock when they reached the railway station where the line to Calcutta began.

Aouda, still in a stupor, was placed in one of the waiting rooms. Mr. Fogg handed Passepartout some money and sent him off to buy clothing and toilet articles for the young woman.

By the time he returned, it was close to the hour for the train for Calcutta to depart. Mr. Fogg paid the Parsee the price·agreed upon and then, to the poor fellow's amazement, presented him with the elephant.

The guide's eyes glistened. "Your honour is giving me a fortune!"

"Parsee," said Mr. Fogg, "you have been loyal and devoted. The animal is yours."

Phileas Fogg, Sir Francis, and Passepartout then assisted Aouda aboard the train and installed her in one of the carriages.

The young woman was beginning to emerge from the influence of the drug. She was a truly beautiful creature, Passepartout observed. She had clear, faultless skin which glowed with the freshness of youth and her eyes had the limpid Indian softness. When she spoke, her English was of the purest.

Aouda was naturally astonished to find herself on a train and in the company of strangers. Sir Francis set about gently telling her what had happened. He dwelt upon the courage Phileas Fogg had shown, risking his life to save her. And he narrated in full the amazing feat by which Passepartout had saved her.

During the story of the rescue, Passepartout blushed and kept muttering, "It isn't worth telling. It isn't worth telling."

While the train whirled toward Benares, Phileas Fogg learned from Aouda that she had a cousin in Hong Kong who was a wealthy merchant. Mr. Fogg assured her that he would escort her to that city where she could remain until the affair at the pagoda of Pillaji had blown over. Aouda gratefully accepted his offer.

At half-past twelve the train reached Benares. There, they exchanged a warm farewell with the gallant brigadier-general, Sir Francis Cromarty. He had proved to be a stout friend.

For the rest of the afternoon and all night long, the train flashed along the track at top speed on the last lap to Calcutta. That city was reached at seven in the morning. As the ship for Hong Kong did not leave until noon, Phileas Fogg had five hours to spare.

According to his journal, he was due in Calcutta on the 25th of October. And he had arrived on that exact date. The two days that had been gained between London and Bombay had been lost. That mattered little to Phileas Fogg.

Nor did it matter to Passepartout. His Gallic soul rejoiced at the romantic conclusion of the adventure which had brought the exotic Aouda to them as a travelling companion. He felt they had left their difficulties behind.

Unfortunately for the hopeful young Frenchman, an individual named Fix had other ideas. Determined to keep Phileas Fogg in India long enough for the arrest warrant to arrive from London, the detective had gone ahead with his scheme to have Mr. Fogg and his servant seized when they reached Calcutta. In fact, at that very moment, Fix was waiting in the Calcutta railway station, his beady eyes inspecting each person who came off the train from Allahabad. Beside Fix stood a stalwart policeman.

It had taken little effort for the detective to convince the Bombay police that a religious law had been broken when Passepartout had tussled with the three priests, and lost his shoes, in the sacred temple at Malabar Hill in Bombay. And an order had been dispatched to Calcutta to have Mr. Fogg and his servant seized. To make sure that there would be no slip-up, Fix had brought the three priests to Calcutta to press charges.

Owing to the delay caused by the rescue of the young widow, Fix and the priests had arrived in Calcutta well ahead of Phileas Fogg and Passepartout. For twenty-four hours the detective had anxiously watched the station, plagued with the thought that the bank robber had escaped.

Suddenly Fix's slight figure stiffened as he caught sight of Mr. Fogg and Passepartout coming from the train. His hand fell heavily on the arm of the policeman.

"There they are," he said hoarsely. "Those two men. I don't know who the woman is but—officer, do your duty."

As the policeman moved forward, Fix slipped away in the crowd, a smile on his face. His plan had worked.

The sudden appearance of the law in the form of a tall and robust policeman startled Passepartout.

"You are Mr. Phileas Fogg?" the policeman asked.

"I am," returned Mr. Fogg.

"And this is your servant?"

"Yes."

"Be so good as to follow me."

"What's the meaning of this?" asked Passepartout.

"You will learn that later," replied the policeman. "Come along."

Mr. Fogg, betraying no surprise, asked if the young lady could accompany them. When permission was granted, they were taken to a carriage and driven to the police station.

Inside, they were escorted to a room with barred windows. "You will appear before the judge in an hour," said the policeman. Then he closed and locked the door.

"We are prisoners!" exclaimed Passepartout. "Prisoners! But why?"

Aouda was distressed. "Sir," she cried to Mr. Fogg, "leave me to my fate. It is on my account that you receive this treatment. It is for having saved me."

Phileas Fogg shook his head. "It is quite unlikely that I would be arrested for preventing a suttee," said he. "There has been some mistake."

"But the steamer," moaned Passepartout. "She leaves at noon!"

"We shall be aboard," replied his master placidly.

After an hour had passed, the policeman unlocked the door and led the prisoners to a courtroom. A fat-faced judge wearing a wig was seated at a desk. At another desk was his clerk, also bewigged.

When the prisoners were identified, the clerk read in a loud voice that Phileas Fogg and his servant were charged with violating the sacred temple of Malabar Hill in Bombay.

Passepartout blinked. Why, that was the place where he'd had the mix-up with those three priests who had stolen his shoes.

"Let the complainants come in," ordered the judge.

A door swung open and the three priests entered. Passepartout glared at them. Violated their temple had he, when he'd been doing just a bit of sightseeing.

"As proof of the charge," droned on the clerk, "here are the very shoes of the person who desecrated the temple."

He placed a pair of shoes on the desk.

"They're mine!" cried Passepartout impulsively.

Hunched down in a shadowy corner at the rear of the courtroom was Fix, the detective. When he heard Passepartout's outburst, a chuckle escaped him. That dunce of a servant. He had as good as confessed to the charge.

"Then the facts are admitted?" asked the judge.

"Admitted," replied Mr. Fogg coldly.

The judge adjusted his wig that had slipped over one eye and pronounced the sentence: "Inasmuch as the English law protects the religions of the Indian people, and as the man Passepartout has admitted that he violated the sacred temple of Malabar Hill, at Bombay, I condemn the said Passepartout to imprisonment for fifteen days and a fine of three hundred pounds."

"Fifteen days," groaned Passepartout. "Three hundred pounds. Oh, no!"

"And inasmuch as the master must be held responsible for the acts of his paid servant," went on the judge, "I condemn Phileas Fogg to a week's imprisonment and a fine of one hundred and fifty pounds."

Passepartout reeled back. A week in jail for Mr. Fogg! This would ruin his master's chance of circling the globe in eighty days. And it had all happened because he, like a fool, had gone into that wretched temple.

"You have that right," replied the judge. "Bail for each prisoner will be one thousand pounds."

"I will pay at once," said Mr. Fogg. He removed a roll of bank notes from the carpetbag, counted out two thousand pounds, and placed them on the clerk's desk.

"This sum will be returned to you on your release from prison," said the judge. "Meanwhile, you are free on bail."

"Come," said Phileas Fogg to Passepartout.

"Let me at least get back my shoes," cried Passepartout. With that he snatched up the footwear and hastened after Mr. Fogg and Aouda.

Fix waited until they had left the courtroom, then quickly followed. The new development had shaken him deeply, yet he tried to convince himself that Phileas Fogg wouldn't be foolish enough to lose two thousand pounds by leaving the country.

Fix, meanwhile, was rubbing his hands gleefully together. With Fogg detained in Calcutta for a week, there would be ample time for the arrest warrant to arrive.

Mr. Fogg did not even lift an eyebrow when the sentence was pronounced. "I offer bail." he said.

from shore. The steamship was the *Rangoon*, and she was scheduled to depart for Hong Kong at noon.

"The rascal is off!" muttered Fix. "He's thrown away two thousand pounds as if it were water. At this rate, the stolen money will soon be gone. He'll have nothing left when he is caught."

The thought chilled Fix. For he had never once forgotten that the detective who arrested the bank robber had been promised five per cent of the money recovered.

"Even so, I'm going after him," Fix resolved. "I'll follow him to the end of the world if necessary."

At once, Fix hastened to book passage on the *Rangoon*. Then, leaving orders for the arrest warrant to be forwarded to him in Hong Kong, he boarded the steamship just a few moments before she raised anchor.

However, after trailing his quarry to the harbour, the detective came face to face with the bitter truth. Fogg had no intention of waiting to serve the sentence. He had hired a small boat and he and his servant and the young woman were being taken out to where a large steamship lay anchored half a mile

A Stormy Voyage

THE *Rangoon* was equipped with sails as well as steam and she was considered a fast boat. But she couldn't go fast enough to suit Passepartout. The confidence the Frenchman had once felt that nothing could stop his master from completing the round-the-world trip in eighty days had been severely shaken by the arrest in Calcutta.

There had been something strange about that arrest. It was almost as if someone had been trying deliberately to slow down Mr. Fogg and make him lose his bet. Of course, such a thing was absurd, Passepartout realized. Yet that didn't relieve his mounting anxiety.

What if some other mishap occurred? What if the *Rangoon* should take longer than eleven days to cross the 3,500 watery miles that lay between Calcutta and Hong Kong? If they failed to arrive by November 5th, the steamer for Yokohama would be missed.

For the first days of the voyage the weather and winds were favourable and the *Rangoon* made good time. Passepartout remained on deck as much as possible. He constantly looked at his large silver watch, which he stubbornly kept at London time, as if an inspection of the moving hands would somehow urge the ship to greater effort.

Phileas Fogg, as usual, appeared completely indifferent to the fact that a wager of twenty thousand pounds lay at the whim of the wind and the waves. He had set aside definite hours for playing whist and for visiting Aouda, a routine he kept with mathematical exactness.

As for the young woman, she constantly expressed her gratitude to her protector. It was soon apparent to Passepartout, from the way Aouda's eyes shyly regarded Mr. Fogg, that she was beginning to feel an emotion stronger than gratitude.

On the 30th of October, the Bay of Bengal was left behind and the *Rangoon* entered the Strait of Malacca that separated the Malay Peninsula from Sumatra. On the following day, the ship was due in Singapore where she would pause briefly for coaling.

During all this time, Fix, the detective, had made it his business to remain out of sight of Passepartout. It might be difficult to explain his presence aboard without awakening the servant's suspicions.

The detective had spent the long hours in his cabin frantically trying to work out some campaign which would successfully bring the bank robber to justice.

The arrest would have to be made in Hong Kong. It was the last English ground on which he would set foot. If Phileas Fogg were allowed to go beyond Hong Kong, to China or Japan or America, a simple arrest warrant would be useless. It would be necessary to have an extradition warrant and that would result in delays and obstacles.

"I have failed at Bombay," Fix muttered to himself. "I have failed at Calcutta. If I fail to arrest Fogg at Hong Kong, the robber will probably be lost forever—and so will my reputation. Cost what may, I *must* succeed. But how can I prevent the rascal's departure from Hong Kong until the arrest warrant arrives?"

The only solution to the vexing problem seemed to be in going to Passepartout and boldly telling him that his master was a criminal and thereby enlisting the servant as an ally. Yet such a procedure might be dangerous. If Passepartout should inform his master that the law was closing in on him, the result would be ruinous.

Deciding to proceed cautiously and feel out the servant first, Fix went on deck that afternoon. Passepartout was walking up and down in the forward part and the detective rushed up to him with every appearance of surprise.

"You here, on the *Rangoon*?" Fix exclaimed.

Passepartout was truly astonished. "Monsieur Fix!" he cried. "I left you at Bombay. Are you going around the world, too?"

"No, no," replied Fix. "I shall stop at Hong Kong for some days."

"But I haven't seen you on board since we left Calcutta."

"I've been staying in my cabin. A touch of seasickness. And how is Mr. Fogg?"

"As well and as punctual as ever, not a day behind time," said Passepartout, delighted to have someone to talk to.

Fix listened carefully as the servant chattered on about the rescue of Aouda and the plan to leave her with a relative in Hong Kong. It was clear that the Frenchman now firmly believed in his master's story of going round the world and was doing everything possible to aid the tour.

"I'd better wait awhile before I tell him the truth," thought Fix. "Perhaps something will happen that will delay this voyage and force Fogg to miss the ship to Yokohama. If he is held up long enough, it won't be necessary to ask for the servant's help."

And something did happen that sent Fix's hopes soaring high.

When the *Rangoon* had completed her coaling at Singapore on October 31st and headed for Hong Kong, the weather turned violent. A gale slashed across the South China Sea, churning up mountainous waves.

The *Rangoon* rolled heavily and was forced to reef all sails. Her speed was cut so drastically that the captain estimated they would reach Hong Kong at least twenty hours behind time unless the storm let up. And it didn't.

Passepartout was furious when he heard the captain's report. Even in the midst of the tempest he remained on deck, shaking his fist and shouting insults at the raging elements.

Once in a while the Frenchman caught brief glimpses of Fix. And Passepartout began to ponder over the strange chance that kept the little man forever turning up along Mr. Fogg's route. The more Passepartout thought about it, the stranger it became, until, suddenly, an explanation struck him.

"He's a spy sent by Monsieur Fogg's friends at the Reform Club!" Passepartout said to himself. "That is surely it! They want to be certain my master really does go round the world. What distrust!"

The Frenchman kept his thoughts to himself, not wishing to disturb his master who would be shocked at such behaviour. But he resolved to keep a sharp eye on Fix.

For four days the storm kept up, lashing the reeling *Rangoon*. At last, on November 4th, calm seas prevailed. The steamship unfurled her sails and sped on. But the captain made it quite evident that the time lost could not be regained. Instead of arriving at Hong Kong on November 5th, they would dock on the 6th. By that time the ship for Yokohama, the *Carnatic*, would have departed. And the next steamer to leave for that Japanese port did not sail for a full week. Clearly, Mr. Fogg was in serious trouble.

the wager, was downcast. But not Phileas Fogg. That worthy gentleman remained as calm as ever.

Then, as the *Rangoon* entered the port of Hong Kong on November 6th and was piloted to her berth, the electrifying news broke. The *Carnatic* had not left for Yokohama after all. She had been forced to wait in Hong Kong while repairs were made to her boilers. Her new sailing time was set for high tide the next morning, November 7th.

This amazing stroke of good fortune threw Passepartout into a spasm of rejoicing. True enough, his master was twenty-four hours behind time. But the *Carnatic* was scheduled to make a direct connection with the steamer that crossed the Pacific to San Francisco. Therefore that ship would not sail from Yokohama until the *Carnatic* arrived.

Passepartout was fairly bouncing when he and Mr. Fogg and Aouda descended the gangway to the dock. He waved merrily to Fix whose scowling face he chanced to see at the ship's rail.

Fix couldn't have been more pleased. In the privacy of his cabin, he rubbed his hands together and did a little jig. At last, luck was on his side. There would be plenty of time for the arrest warrant to reach him now.

Passepartout was seething with indignation. Even Aouda, who had been told about the dash round the world and

Foul Play in Hong Kong

MR. FOGG summoned a carriage and they proceeded to the Club Hotel where rooms were engaged for the night. After making sure that Aouda was comfortable and instructing Passepartout to remain at the hotel, Mr. Fogg set out in search of the young woman's cousin. He went directly to the Exchange where he believed someone would know of the whereabouts of the wealthy cotton merchant.

Meeting a broker who had been acquainted with the merchant, Phileas Fogg learned that Aouda's cousin had retired from business two years ago and had gone to Holland to live.

When Mr. Fogg returned with this news, Aouda passed a hand across her forehead. "What ought I to do, Mr. Fogg?" she asked in her soft voice.

"It is very simple," responded Phileas Fogg. "Go on to Europe with us."

"But I cannot intrude . . ."

"You do not intrude in the least," said Mr. Fogg. He turned to Passepartout. "Proceed to the *Carnatic* and engage three cabins."

Passepartout hurried off, delighted that the young woman was to continue the journey with them.

On reaching the dock where the *Carnatic* was moored, Passepartout was not surprised to find Fix walking up and down. Nor was the detective surprised to see the Frenchman. In fact, Fix had come there in the hope of running into Phileas Fogg's servant.

With the abrupt turn of fortune, the detective's situation was critical. As he had feared, the arrest warrant had not arrived. Now the only way to stop the robber Fogg from departing on the *Carnatic* seemed to be to tell the servant the truth about his master and ask for his help. If that did not work, something more drastic would have to be done.

Passepartout smiled to himself when he saw the detective. What a blow this delay of the *Carnatic* was for those gentlemen of the Reform Club and their spy. It amused the Frenchman highly that he had guessed the true identity of Fix.

"Well, Monsieur Fix," said Passepartout, "have you decided not to remain in Hong Kong after all but to go along with us to America?"

"Perhaps," said Fix.

Passepartout laughed. "I knew you would not wish to separate yourself from us," said he, slyly. "You were only going to Bombay and here you are in China. America is not far off. And from America to Europe is only a step."

Fix was puzzled by the remark. Had the servant somehow discovered that he was a detective? If so, had he told his master? Indeed, was it possible that this Frenchman was not a servant at all, but an accomplice of the bank robber?

"Come and engage your berth," said Passepartout.

"Very well," said Fix. It might be wise to do what the servant suggested. For if he failed to keep Phileas Fogg in Hong Kong, Fix was determined to remain on his trail.

The two men entered the steamship office together and secured cabins for four persons. The clerk, as he gave them the tickets, informed them that the repairs on the *Carnatic* had been completed. The steamer would leave that very evening instead of the next morning.

"That will suit my master all the better," said Passepartout. "I shall go and tell him at once."

At the clerk's words, Fix's heart had given a skip and a jump. What if the servant was somehow kept from notifying Phileas Fogg of this last-minute change in the sailing time? Might not the robber wait until the following morning to board the *Carnatic*, only to find that she had gone?

It was a scheme that might work, Fix excitedly told himself. But first he would try persuasion on the servant.

As they left the dock area together, the detective spied a nearby tavern.

"Allow me to buy you a glass of wine," said he to Passepartout.

The idea appealed to Passepartout, for he was very thirsty. "Thank you, Monsieur Fix," said he. "But I must not remain too long."

On entering the tavern, they found themselves in a large room where a number of men were seated at small tables. Passepartout and Fix sat down at an unoccupied one and the detective ordered two bottles of wine.

Little was said as they drank. When the bottles were empty, Passepartout started to get to his feet.

"I must inform my master of the change in the *Carnatic's* sailing time," said he.

Fix caught him by the arm. "Wait a moment," he said. "I want to have a serious talk with you about your master." As he spoke, he motioned for the waiter to bring more wine.

Fix filled Passepartout's wine glass. Then lowering his voice he said, "You have guessed who I am?"

"Indeed, I have," said Passepartout. "Not that I have told my master. He would be shocked to learn that his fellow members of the Reform Club have hired you to trail him. Monsieur Fogg is an honest man. When he makes a wager, he tries to win it fairly."

Fix was puzzled. "I don't know what you're talking about. No club hired me. I'm a police detective."

Passepartout almost choked on his wine. "A detective!" he gasped.

"Here is my commission," said Fix. He produced the official document.

Passepartout stared at it, speechless.

"If you are a detective, why are you following Monsieur Fogg?" he asked.

Fix leaned across the table. "Listen," said he. And he quickly told Passepartout about the Bank of England robbery by a person whose description tallied exactly with that of Phileas Fogg.

"Nonsense," said Passepartout. "My master is the most honourable of men!"

How can you tell? You scarcely know him. This tale of making a bet was just an excuse so that he could leave London in a hurry without suspicion. The large amount in banknotes he carries is stolen money."

"No! No!" cried Passepartout. "I will not believe it."

"Would you like to be arrested as his accomplice?" asked Fix.

Shocked, Passepartout reached for his glass, which the detective had again refilled, and drank its contents. What horror was this? Surely, it was all a bad dream.

"If you want to avoid trouble," went on the detective, "you will help me keep Mr. Fogg here in Hong Kong for a day or so until I receive the warrant for his arrest which is being forwarded to me from Calcutta. Do this and I promise to share with you the two-thousand-pound reward offered by the bank."

"Never!" exclaimed Passepartout. He tried to rise but fell back. "Even if what you say is true, I will never betray my master—no, not for all the gold in the world."

Fix eyed the Frenchman carefully. In his agitation, Passepartout had been draining his glass as fast as Mr. Fix filled it. The wine was already having its effect.

"Very well then," said the detective. "I respect you as a true and loyal servant. Forget all I have said and let us drink to our health."

So upset was Passepartout at what had been told him that he offered no resistance when Fix continued to refill his glass. The detective, however, consumed very little wine.

After a while Passepartout yawned.

His eyes grew heavy and finally they closed. With a deep sigh, poor Passepartout slumped unconscious across the table.

Fix arose at once and, calling the manager of the tavern, paid the bill.

"Perhaps you might have a room where my friend could sleep," said he, offering the manager an extra banknote.

The tavern keeper winked. "We'll look after him, your honour," said he.

Fix left the tavern, a spring to his step. If Phileas Fogg did not get wind of the change in the *Carnatic's* sailing from some other source, all would be well.

Tempest in the China Seas

WHILE these events were taking place at the tavern, Phileas Fogg was quietly escorting Aouda on a tour of the shops It was all very well for an Englishman to make a trip around the world with a carpetbag. But a lady could not be expected to do so.

After numerous items for Aouda's wardrobe had been purchased, Mr. Fogg and the young woman returned to the hotel. There they dined in a leisurely fashion. Following dinner, Aouda retired to her room for the night while Mr. Fogg set about reading English newspapers and magazines.

Believing that the *Carnatic* was not due to leave for Yokohama until the next morning, Phileas Fogg was not disturbed when his servant failed to re-

turn by bedtime. Even when Passepartout did not appear in answer to his master's bell the next morning, Mr. Fogg betrayed not the slightest sign of vexation. Instead, he ordered the newly acquired luggage sent to the *Carnatic*. Then, calling Aouda, he and the young woman took a carriage to the dock where they arrived shortly after eight o'clock.

Mr. Fogg had expected to find not only the steamer but his servant. When neither was present, he showed no trace of surprise.

"Where is Passepartout?" cried Aouda. "Where is the *Carnatic*?"

"The ship apparently has sailed," said Phileas Fogg placidly. "As for Passepartout, I know not."

At that moment, Fix, who had been loitering nearby, wiped the smirk off his face and approached.

"Pardon me, sir," said he, "but I thought I would find your servant here."

"We have not seen him since yester-day," said Aouda. "Could he have gone on board the *Carnatic* without us?"

"Did you intend to sail on the *Carnatic*?"

"Yes, indeed."

"So did I, madam," said Fix. "And I am deeply disappointed. The *Carnatic*, its repairs completed, left Hong Kong twelve hours before the stated time, without any notice being given. We must now wait a week for another steamer."

The detective chuckled to himself. In a day or so the warrant would be in his hands and the slippery robber, Fogg, would be in jail.

But Fix's feeling of joy was abruptly replaced by one of horror when he heard Phileas Fogg say, casually, "There are other vessels besides the *Carnatic* in the harbour of Hong Kong. Let us find one."

With that, Mr. Fogg offered his arm to Aouda and together they went off to look for an available craft. Stunned, Fix trailed along. If only the search would result in failure.

It took considerable time, going first to one vessel then to another. But within three hours, Mr. Fogg had come upon a pilot boat, the *Tankadere*, that could be hired.

Phileas Fogg spoke to the master, a man named John Bunsby.

"I have missed the *Carnatic*," said Mr. Fogg, "and I must get to Yoko-hama by the 14th at the latest to catch the steamer for San Francisco. I offer you one hundred pounds per day and an additional reward of two hundred pounds if I reach Yokohama in time."

John Bunsby shook his head. "I am sorry, your honour," said he. "I could not risk myself, my men, or my little boat of scarcely twenty tons on so long a voyage at this time of year. Besides, we could not reach Yokohama in time, for it is sixteen hundred and sixty miles from Hong Kong."

Fix breathed more easily. The robber's efforts were going to fail, after all.

"But," added John Bunsby, "there is another way your voyage might be arranged."

"How?" asked Mr. Fogg.

"By going to Shanghai, which is only eight hundred miles from here."

"Mr. Bunsby," said Mr. Fogg, "I must take the American steamer at Yokohama and not at Shanghai."

"Why?" returned John Bunsby. "The San Francisco steamer does not start from Yokohama. It puts in at Yokohama, true enough, but it starts from Shanghai."

"You are certain of that?"

"Perfectly. The American steamer, the *General Grant*, leaves Shanghai on November 11th, at seven in the evening."

"We would have, therefore, four days," said Phileas Fogg. "That is, ninety-six hours."

"Yes, your honour," said the master of the *Tankadere*. "In that time, if we have good luck and a southwest wind and the sea is calm, we could make the eight hundred miles to Shanghai."

"How soon could we leave?" asked Mr. Fogg.

"In an hour, directly provisions can be got aboard."

Phileas Fogg turned to Aouda. "You would not be afraid to go, would you, madam?"

"Not with you, Mr. Fogg," was her answer.

"Then it is a bargain," said Mr. Fogg to John Bunsby. "Here are two hundred pounds on account."

All during the conversation, Fix had stood listening in an agony of despair. If that confounded arrest warrant had only shown up. But now, even if it came tomorrow, it would be too late. Fogg would have left English soil.

The detective bit at his lower lip. Should he abandon the bank robber? His very soul rebelled at the thought. It was his duty never to lose sight of Fogg until he could bring the rascal to justice. How could he do that now?

Phileas Fogg, himself, gave the answer. He directed his gaze at Fix and said, "If you would like to take advantage of this opportunity to go to Yokohama, you may sail with us."

"Thank you, sir," said the detective in a most surprised voice.

"In half an hour we shall go aboard," said Mr. Fogg.

"But what about poor Passepartout?" exclaimed Aouda, who was much distressed by the servant's disappearance.

"I shall do what I can to find him," replied Phileas Fogg.

While Fix boarded the *Tankadere*, Mr. Fogg and Aouda visited the Hong Kong police station in the hope that they might have a report of Passepartout. Learning that the police had heard nothing, Mr. Fogg left a sum of money to be spent in searching for the Frenchman. Then, having had the luggage brought to the *Tankadere*, Phileas Fogg and the young woman joined Fix aboard the vessel.

The *Tankadere* was a neat little craft as gracefully built as a racing yacht.

"I'm sorry to have nothing better to offer you," said Mr. Fogg to Fix.

The detective had a slight feeling of shame. It did not seem right to accept favours from the very man he planned to arrest.

"Though he is a rascal," thought Fix, "he is a polite one."

At ten minutes past three on the afternoon of November 7th, the sails were hoisted and the *Tankadere* bounded briskly forward over the waves.

The voyage of eight hundred miles up the perilous coast of China proved to be a rough and turbulent one.

November 9th passed with the waves buffeting the *Tankadere* cruelly. At noon on November 10th, the tempest began to wear itself out and by the next morning, November 11th, the storm was gone.

The ship's master stated that they were within one hundred miles of Shanghai.

"It will be nip and tuck if we make it by seven o'clock tonight when the *General Grant* departs," said John Bunsby to Phileas Fogg.

At noon, the *Tankadere* was within forty-five miles of Shanghai. By six o'clock that afternoon the craft was within ten miles of the mouth of the Shanghai River. At seven o'clock they were still three miles short.

John Bunsby's lips were set in a tight line. They were going to be too late. It was then that Phileas Fogg made an idle motion with his hand, pointing ahead.

The long black funnel of a large steamship had appeared on the horizon.

"The *General Grant*," said Phileas Fogg. "Direct your craft across her path, Mr. Bunsby. Then hoist your flag to half-mast and fire your cannon."

The master of the *Tankadere* did as directed. The flag was run halfway up the mast in a signal of distress. The small cannon which stood on the forward deck for signalling in bad weather was touched off with a red-hot coal.

As the cannon's boom resounded through the air, Mr. Fogg said, "Unless I am mistaken, the captain of the *General Grant* will observe our distress signal and direct his course toward us."

The calculations of Mr. Fogg proved correct. A short while later, the American steamship hove to while the *Tankadere* came alongside. Using a megaphone, Mr. Bunsby shouted out his passengers' predicament to the captain of the *General Grant* who consented to take them aboard.

After paying the agreed-upon price to the master of the *Tankadere*, with an additional sum of five hundred and fifty pounds, Phileas Fogg followed Aouda and Fix up the ladder on the side of the *General Grant*.

"You did it, Mr. Fogg!" exclaimed Aouda when they had the solid deck of the American ship under their feet. "I would be supremely happy if I only knew where Passepartout was."

"I feel that he is quite safe," said Phileas Fogg. "Perhaps he is, even now, aboard the *Carnatic* proceeding to Yokohama. Let us hope so."

Passepartout Is Found

PASSEPARTOUT was, indeed, aboard the steamship *Carnatic*, although his memory of exactly how he had got there was somewhat cloudy. And with good reason.

Three hours or so after Fix had left him in the tavern sprawled across the table, Passepartout awakened to find himself lying on a cot in a back room.

With the one idea in his befuddled brain of getting aboard the *Carnatic* and joining his master and Aouda, Passepartout left the tavern and directed his wavering steps toward the dock. Reeling and falling, he somehow managed to reach the steamship which was on the point of departure.

Just as the gangway was about to be pulled in, Passepartout stumbled across it and fell unconscious on the deck. Several sailors picked him up and carried him to a cabin.

When the Frenchman awoke the next morning, he was startled to learn that they were already one hundred and fifty miles from Hong Kong. The salt air sobered him and as he began to collect his wits, he wondered fearfully what Monsieur Fogg would say about his dreadful behaviour. The only thing to do was to go to his master and apologize.

But although he searched everywhere, he could find no trace of either Phileas Fogg or Aouda. It was only when he consulted the purser and learned that they were not on the passenger list that the awful truth struck him.

He had failed to inform his master that the time of sailing had been changed. They had missed the ship.

Passepartout sunk down in a deck chair and held his head in his hands. Fix had been responsible for this. In order to detain Mr. Fogg in Hong Kong that traitor had tricked him into getting drunk.

What a fiend! Mr. Fogg was now ruined, his bet lost. Moreover he was perhaps arrested and imprisoned.

Passepartout tore at his hair in his despair. If Fix ever came within his reach, what a settling of accounts there would be.

After a while, the Frenchman began to study his own situation. It was certainly not a happy one. Here he was on his way to Japan but what would he do when he got there? His pockets were empty. He had not so much as a penny. Fortunately his passage, which included meals, had been paid for in advance. But after that . . .

For the next few days, Passepartout ate heartily at every opportunity, endeavouring to store up enough food for the bleak and uncertain future.

At dawn on November 13th the *Carnatic* entered the port of Yokohama. After the steamship had anchored at the dock, Passepartout went timidly ashore.

Having nothing else to do, he wandered aimlessly through the city. The streets were crowded with strangely garbed people, and Passepartout was fascinated. Toward evening, having walked all day, his feet began to hurt. Moreover, despite the huge breakfast he had eaten aboard the *Carnatic*, the pangs of hunger were upon him.

Finally, as darkness descended, he came again to the harbour and, feeling utterly miserable and forlorn, Passepartout sank down in a doorway to sleep.

The next morning when he awakened, his hunger was acute. He could, of course, sell his precious silver watch but he would rather starve to death. Returning to the Japanese quarter, he came upon a dealer in old clothes and he conceived the idea that he might be able to trade his clothes for a native costume and some money to boot.

The dealer was delighted with the European clothes, and the transaction was successfully accomplished. A short while later Passepartout emerged from the shop clad in an ancient Japanese costume. A few small pieces of silver jingled in his pocket and his usually happy expression had returned.

He soon entered a teahouse where he spent his money feasting on half a bird and some rice.

"Now," he thought, "I must consider how to leave this country. Perhaps I might be hired as a cook or a servant aboard one of the American steamers. If I can but proceed to San Francisco, some way will be found to go on from there."

Even as the thought was passing through his head, Passepartout noticed a man dressed as a clown walking down the street. The man carried a large sign on which was printed in English:

ACROBATIC JAPANESE TROUPE
Last Performance Before Departure
For The United States
GREAT ATTRACTION
HONOURABLE WILLIAM BATULCAR
Manager

The troupe was going to the United States! That meant free passage.

Passepartout excitedly followed the man bearing the sign and came to a building whose walls were covered with posters advertising the company of jugglers.

Entering the place, Passepartout was directed to the manager, Mr. Batulcar.

"What do you want?" asked Mr. Batulcar, gazing at the strangely adorned creature before him. "You are no more a Japanese than I am a monkey."

"I am a Frenchman," said Passepartout. "A Parisian of Paris. I would like to find a place in your troupe. I have been a circus rider and a gymnast."

"You have strong muscles?"

"Especially after a good meal."

"Humph," said Mr. Batulcar. "It happens that I need a pair of sturdy shoulders for the human pyramid. The fellow who had the job quit. You're hired."

Passepartout was overcome. He had found a job and soon he would be on his way to San Francisco.

The final performance of the acrobatic troupe was to begin at three o'clock. There was no time for Passepartout to rehearse his part, but that worried him little. As a gymnast, he had done this sort of thing before. It would take considerable strength, of course, for he was to be one of the key men at the base of the pyramid which was formed by a succession of other performers rising above.

Before three o'clock had arrived, the theatre was packed with spectators and a Japanese orchestra began playing.

Standing in the wings, Passepartout watched the performance begin. It was like all acrobatic displays. There were amazing juggling feats, fantastic feats of balance. Act followed act until finally it was time for the climax, the human pyramid.

At the signal, Passepartout trotted out on the stage and took his place with the other performers who were to form the base of the pyramid. A second group of acrobats climbed up on their shoulders. A third mounted their shoulders. Then a fourth and a fifth, until a human monument reached the very top of the stage.

While Passepartout was thus occupied in supporting a tower of humanity, it so happened that Phileas Fogg and Aouda entered the theatre. They had reached Yokohama that very morning, November 14th, and Mr. Fogg and the young woman had lost no time in boarding the *Carnatic* to learn, if possible, what had happened to their travelling companion.

The ship's purser had informed them that a Frenchman named Passepartout had, indeed, arrived on the *Carnatic* the day before. Straightaway, Mr. Fogg and Aouda had begun a search of the city. When visits to the French and English consuls had brought no news of Passepartout, they walked the streets in the hope of catching sight of the missing servant.

Some whim of fate had guided their steps so that they had entered the theatre where the acrobatic troupe was performing, right at the moment of the show's climax.

On the stage the last man, at the very pinnacle of the human pyramid, had taken his place and the audience burst into loud applause.

It was then that Passepartout chanced to look out beyond the footlights. In utter amazement he saw Monsieur Fogg and Aouda standing at the rear.

A cry of pure joy was wrung from Passepartout's lips. His master was here. He must join him at once.

Quite forgetting his responsibility to others, Passepartout made for the edge of the stage. The result of his abrupt movement was shattering.

The human pyramid trembled. The man at the top waved his arms wildly as he tried to recover his balance. His fellows below him swayed and tottered like a ship in a heavy sea. Then, with the keystone removed from the base, the pyramid collapsed.

Performers, kicking and struggling, cascaded through the air. A volley of heart-rending cries filled the packed theatre. In a flash, the human structure which had been so impressive was gone, and the stage was strewn with a tangled heap of writhing acrobats.

Passepartout did not care. He cleared the footlights in a leap and ran up the aisle shouting, "My master! My master!"

Mr. Fogg gave no sign of surprise at all. "Let us go, young man," he said curtly, and turned on his heel.

Mr. Batulcar, furious with rage at Passepartout, tried to bar their passage, demanding damages for the breakage of the pyramid. Mr. Fogg coldly gave him a handful of banknotes and, escorting Aouda on his arm, stalked from the place. Passepartout trotted behind.

That evening of November 14th, with Phileas Fogg, Aouda, and Passepartout aboard, the American steamship *General Grant* took to the high seas for her trip across the wide Pacific to San Francisco.

Insult in San Francisco

THE *General Grant* was a paddle-wheel steamer of two thousand tons, well equipped and very fast. It seemed reasonable to Phileas Fogg that he could expect to reach San Francisco by the 2nd of December, New York by the 11th, and London on the 20th. This would give him a day to spare before he was due to walk into the Reform Club at a quarter to nine P.M. on the fateful day of December 21st.

Passepartout, also, had complete faith that his master's round-the-world journey would be completed in eighty days. But bitter experience, such as he had had at the hands of Fix, had taught him not to expect everything to run smoothly.

Just the thought of the detective caused Passepartout's eyes to glint with anger. The Frenchman had made no mention of Fix when he had explained to Mr. Fogg about the incident in the Hong Kong tavern. He had simply con-

fessed that he had foolishly drunk too much wine, and let it go at that. Passepartout was determined to handle Monsieur Fix in his own way if that sly individual ever turned up again.

The chance of such a happening was closer than Passepartout could imagine. Fix was, at that very moment, a passenger on the *General Grant.*

At Yokohama, the detective had gone directly to the British consulate where, to his amazement, he had found the arrest warrant. It had followed him from Bombay to Calcutta and then to Hong Kong. There the police, learning that Fix had gone on to Yokohama, had placed it on a fast ship and sped it to the Japanese city.

The detective had raged at the injustice of fate. If only the document had arrived while Phileas Fogg had been under English law at Hong Kong! It was useless in Japan.

69

"However," Fix had thought, "the rogue evidently intends to return to England. Well, I'll follow him there and use the warrant the minute he steps ashore."

Fix had then gone back to the *General Grant* and purchased a ticket to San Francisco. He had been on deck when, in the distance, he had chanced to see Mr. Fogg and Aouda coming along the dock and with them Passepartout.

For a moment the detective had stared unbelieving at the man he had abandoned in Hong Kong. Then he had retreated to his cabin and remained there, coming out only rarely.

But even though Fix tried his best to stay out of Passepartout's way, they finally met.

It happened at noon on the 23rd of November, the day when the *General Grant* crossed the 180th meridian and was therefore exactly half way round the world from London.

Passepartout was standing on deck holding his silver watch whose hands he had persistently refused to change. He had just made the discovery that his watch agreed exactly with the ship's timepieces, not knowing that although it was twelve noon in the Pacific, it was twelve midnight in London.

"All this talk about changing time," thought Passepartout. "What rot! I knew the sun would some day regulate itself by my watch."

The Frenchman had just returned his precious watch to his pocket when he looked up and beheld the detective, Fix.

Without a word, Passepartout rushed at Fix and knocked him to the deck.

Even though his senses reeled from the attack, Fix was thinking rapidly. The task of following Phileas Fogg would be most difficult if this raging Frenchman continued to show opposition. Somehow he would have to pacify the angry servant.

"Enough," said Fix. "Let me have a word with you."

"I've already had too many," retorted Passepartout.

"It is in your master's interest," said Fix, rising painfully to his feet.

A crowd of passengers had begun to gather and Fix moved away to a secluded section of the ship. Passepartout reluctantly followed, his fists still doubled up.

"Well, what is it?" asked Passepartout sharply.

"You have given me a thrashing," said Fix. "I expected it. Now listen to me. I have been Mr. Fogg's foe but now I am on his side."

"Bah!" said Passepartout. "I do not believe it."

Fix chose his words carefully. "As long as Mr. Fogg was under English law, as he was in India and in Hong Kong, it was my duty to arrest him," said the detective smoothly. "Now that he has removed himself from such territory, my arrest warrant is useless. I will, therefore, do nothing to impede his progress—in fact, I will do my utmost to see that he gets to England."

Passepartout listened carefully. It seemed to him that Fix spoke in good faith. But he could not be certain.

"There is no reason to consider me an enemy now, is there?" asked Fix.

"Perhaps not," replied Passepartout. "But at the first sign of treason, I will twist your neck for you."

"Agreed," said the detective.

The voyage across the Pacific turned out to be smooth and uneventful. Ten days later, on the 3rd of December, the *General Grant* entered the bay of the Golden Gate and reached San Francisco.

Phileas Fogg had neither gained nor lost a single day.

It was seven in the morning when Mr. Fogg, Aouda, and Passepartout set foot upon the American continent. Learning that the first train for New York left at six that evening, Phileas Fogg hailed a carriage and directed the driver to take them to the International Hotel.

After breakfast, Passepartout proposed that he purchase a dozen rifles and revolvers. He had heard many stories of how American trains were attacked by bands of Indians. Mr. Fogg thought this a useless precaution, but he gave his servant money and told him to go ahead if he wished.

Then Phileas Fogg and Aouda set out for the English consulate to have his passport visaed. Directly this had been accomplished, they were starting on an inspection of the city when they happened to run into Fix.

The detective acted most surprised. What! Had he and Mr. Fogg crossed the Pacific together without meeting on the steamer. How amazing!

"Business has recalled me to Europe, sir," said Fix glibly. "I would be honoured if I could continue the rest of the trip in your company."

Mr. Fogg bowed stiffly. "The honour is mine," said he.

Then, in order not to lose sight of the bank robber, Fix begged permission to accompany Mr. Fogg and Aouda on their stroll about San Francisco.

"Pray do so," said Phileas Fogg cordially.

They soon found themselves in Montgomery Street where a great crowd was collected. Men were going about carrying large posters and flags while loud cries were heard on all sides.

"Hurrah for Camerfield!"

"Hurrah for Mandiboy!"

"This must be a political meeting," said Fix. "Perhaps we had better not mingle with the crowd. There may be danger. I have heard these Americans take their politics so seriously that they often resort to fisticuffs."

Just as they were about to withdraw, there was an unusual stir in the human mass. Angry shouts arose. Canes were raised and brought down sharply. The din of voices grew deafening.

Before Mr. Fogg, Aouda, and Fix could escape, the street fight surged around them. Phileas Fogg held Aouda close to him, trying to protect her.

At that moment a brawny red-bearded fellow charged past, jolting Mr. Fogg so hard that he almost fell.

"Take care," said Phileas Fogg.

The man turned angrily and raised his fist. He was about to give Mr. Fogg a crushing blow when Fix rushed in. The man's fist hit the detective instead and promptly knocked him down.

"Yankee!" exclaimed Mr. Fogg. "I told you to take care!"

"So, an Englishman!" returned the brawny fellow. "I'll take care of *you*. We will meet again."

"When you please," said Mr. Fogg, his voice cold.

"What is your name?"

"Phileas Fogg. And yours?"

"Colonel Stamp Proctor."

The human tide now swept by, taking with it the red-bearded man. Fix got to his feet. He was bruised but not seriously hurt.

"Thank you," said Mr. Fogg to the detective.

"No thanks are necessary," replied Fix. "But let us get out of here."

from Colonel Proctor's blow, Passepartout's countenance cleared. It seemed evident that Fix was indeed no longer an enemy.

Following dinner that night, as they were leaving for the station, Mr. Fogg said to Fix, "Have you seen this Colonel Proctor again?"

"No," replied Fix.

"I will come back to America to find him some day," said Phileas Fogg calmly. "As an Englishman, I cannot permit myself to be treated as I was this morning without defending my honour."

Later, when the travellers were about to enter the train, Mr. Fogg called to the conductor: "Was there not some trouble today in San Francisco?"

"Just a political meeting, sir," replied the conductor.

"The election of a President, no doubt?" asked Mr. Fogg.

"No, sir," said the conductor. "A justice of the peace."

Passepartout was waiting at the hotel when they returned. The Frenchman frowned as his eyes fell on Fix. But after Aouda told him about their adventure and how Fix had saved Phileas Fogg

Wild Dash to New York

PASSEPARTOUT was never to forget that wild dash across the United States of America. The train left San Francisco at six o'clock at night. Two hours later, a porter entered the car and, in a few minutes, it was transformed into a dormitory. The seats were converted into bunks and shielded by thick curtains.

Amazed at the ingenious system, Passepartout stretched out and was soon asleep. During the night California was left behind. By morning they were in Nevada. A stop was made for a late breakfast at Reno, then the journey continued.

Passepartout stayed close to the window, fascinated by the varied landscape that whisked by: vast prairies with mountains lining the horizon, foaming rivers. Sometimes a great herd of buffalo could be seen.

To the Frenchman the rumble of the wheels seemed to go on for ever. He lost count of time. He ate. He slept. He ate again. Mr. Fogg had discovered that Fix could play whist, as could Aouda. A pack of cards was purchased from the porter and a game was started.

The game went on and on, with pauses only for meals and for sleep at night. Through the Humboldt Range the train progressed, on into Utah with its Great Salt Lake. Then they were in Wyoming. It began to snow, and Passepartout grew fearful that it might block the locomotive and cause delay. But the train chugged on.

Thirteen hundred and eighty-two miles had been passed in three days and three nights. Four days and four nights more would bring them to New York. Phileas Fogg was not yet behind time.

They entered Nebraska and touched at Julesburg, on the southern branch of the Platte River. At eight o'clock in the morning Fort McPherson had come and gone. Three hundred and fifty-seven miles had still to be covered before they would be in Omaha.

Mr. Fogg and his partners had resumed their game of whist. During the morning, chance was favouring Phileas Fogg. He was on the point of playing a spade when a voice spoke from behind him: "I would play a diamond."

Mr. Fogg, Aouda, and Fix raised their heads. Passepartout, who was gazing out the window across the aisle, turned to see who had spoken.

It was Colonel Stamp Proctor, the man who had insulted Phileas Fogg in San Francisco!

Aouda's face went pale. To think that this terrible person should be on this very train. Fear came into her eyes.

Mr. Fogg calmly regarded Colonel Proctor. Then he tossed down the ten of spades. "*I* prefer a spade," said he.

Colonel Proctor made a movement as if to seize the cards. "You know nothing about whist, Englishman!"

Phileas Fogg rose to his feet in spite of Aouda's frantic clutch at his arm. "Colonel Stamp Proctor has again insulted me. He shall give me satisfaction."

"Any time, any place, any weapons," replied the Colonel.

"Sir," said Mr. Fogg, "I am in a great hurry to get back to Europe. Will you agree to a meeting six months hence?"

"It's now or never," sneered Colonel Proctor. "The train will stop at the next station, Plum Creek, for ten minutes. In those ten minutes, several revolver shots could be exchanged."

"Very well," said Mr. Fogg. "I will meet you at Plum Creek."

"And you'll stay there," added the Colonel with a sneer.

The conductor had paused on his way past. "You can't get off at Plum Creek, gentlemen. We are twenty minutes late and we aren't stopping."

"But I am to fight a duel with this person," said Mr. Fogg.

"Why not fight as we go along?" suggested the conductor. "I'll clear out the rear car. You can use that."

This being agreeable to both parties, preparations were made. The few passengers in the end car were asked to

move. Colonel Proctor took a position at one end of the long aisle. Phileas Fogg stood at the other end. Each grasped a revolver. They were to begin firing at the first whistle of the locomotive.

Passepartout, who was acting as his master's second, and an American, who was serving in the same capacity for Colonel Proctor, remained outside with the door closed. Passepartout's heart was beating wildly. He strained his ears to catch the first screech of the engine's whistle.

Suddenly, from up ahead, savage cries resounded in the air and there was the sound of shooting. The firing had certainly not come from the car where the duel was to take place.

Soon the horrifying truth became known. The train was being attacked by a band of Sioux Indians. They raced alongside on their horses and leaped aboard. The engineer and the stoker had been knocked unconscious. An Indian, trying to stop the train, had yanked the steam-valve open instead of closing it. The locomotive was now tearing along the track at a terrific speed.

Colonel Proctor and Mr. Fogg postponed their duel and, revolvers in hand, rushed forward to try to repel the Indians. Passepartout went with them.

Many of the Sioux had invaded the cars and were fighting hand-to-hand with the passengers. Aouda had snatched up a revolver and was courageously defending herself. Fix, too, was making use of Passepartout's arsenal.

In the brief but bloody encounter twenty Sioux fell mortally wounded and a number of passengers lay shot or stunned. The conductor was fighting beside Mr. Fogg when he was hit.

"Unless the train is stopped in five minutes," cried he, "we are lost!"

Fort Kearney, with its garrison of soldiers, was only two miles ahead. If the train went beyond that, the Sioux would be master of the situation.

"It shall be stopped," said Phileas Fogg, preparing to rush forward.

"I will go," cried Passepartout.

The Frenchman, unseen by the Indians, opened a door and slipped under the car just ahead. With acrobatic agility, Passepartout crept underneath one carriage after another, until he had reached the forward end of the train.

There, suspended by one hand between the baggage car and the tender, he managed to disconnect the train from the engine. The locomotive raced ahead while the carriages slowed down and finally came to a stop, less than a hundred feet from Fort Kearney.

The soldiers of the fort, warned by the shooting, came rushing up. The Sioux immediately took to their horses and rode away.

When the passengers were counted on the station platform, three men were missing, among them the courageous Passepartout. A soldier reported that he had seen a man crawl out from under the front carriage when it stopped. At that moment, a Sioux chieftain had dashed by on his horse. He had reached down, seized the man, and flung him across the saddle.

Instantly Phileas Fogg reached a decision. "I will find Passepartout, even if it means the defeat of my trip!"

"Ah, Mr. Fogg," said Aouda.

Thirty soldiers volunteered to aid Mr. Fogg. Just before the expedition set out, Phileas Fogg said to Fix, "Please remain here with Aouda in case anything should happen to me."

Then, after pressing the young woman's hand, Mr. Fogg joined the band of soldiers and the troop moved off across the snow-covered plains in the direction the Sioux had taken.

Aouda retired to a waiting room in the station and there she sat, dwelling on the courage and sacrifice of her protector. Fix, however, was plagued with different thoughts. Like a fool, he had allowed himself to be separated from the bank robber. What if Mr. Fogg did not return?

At two o'clock that afternoon, the locomotive that had been cut loose from the train came backing down the track. It had run on some twenty miles before coming to a stop when the fuel had burned low. There the engineer and stoker had recovered their senses and were now returning to rescue the carriages that had been left behind.

As soon as the engine was hooked again to the rest of the train, the passengers began entering the carriages.

Aouda hurried to the conductor. "Is the train leaving?" she asked.

"At once, madam."

"But the prisoners, our unfortunate fellow travellers . . ."

"I cannot wait. We are already three hours behind time."

"When will another train from San Francisco pass here?"

"Tomorrow evening, madam. If you wish to go with us, please get in."

"I will not go," said Aouda.

The train pulled out, bearing some of the wounded, among them Colonel Proctor, whose injuries were serious. Aouda and Fix watched it leave. Even if Mr. Fogg returned safely with Passepartout, he could never get to New York now in time to catch the steamer for Liverpool.

Snow began falling heavily and it grew very cold. As the hours passed, Aouda kept coming out of the waiting room to peer through the white tempest, hoping to catch sight of Phileas Fogg and the soldiers.

By evening the little band had not returned. The night passed. Dawn came and still there was no sign of the rescue party. Then at seven o'clock gunshots were heard. Was it a signal? It was. For there, half a mile away, the expedition was returning in good order.

At the head came Phileas Fogg, followed by Passepartout and the other two missing travellers. They were welcomed with joyful shouts by the soldiers from the fort. The Sioux had been tracked down and, after a vicious fight, the prisoners had been rescued.

Aouda clung to Mr. Fogg's arm, too moved to speak.

Meanwhile Passepartout was looking about him. "The train! Where is the train?" he asked.

"Gone," said Fix.

"When does the next one pass here?" asked Phileas Fogg.

"Not until this evening."

"Ah," said the impassive Mr. Fogg.

It was, oddly enough, Fix who lit the flame of hope again. Determined to get the robber to England so that he could use the arrest warrant, the detective had made inquiries for some means of transportation to the railway centre of Omaha.

He had been referred to a man named Mudge who owned a curious vehicle. It was a type of iceboat, a sledge rigged like a sloop with a high mast to which large sails were attached. Such iceboats, Fix learned, were able to make rapid journeys across the frozen plains and were frequently used during the winter when the trains were blocked by snow.

Phileas Fogg lost not a moment when Fix informed him of the iceboat. As soon as he saw that it was large enough to carry five or six persons, Mr. Fogg immediately made a bargain with Mudge, the owner, to take them to Omaha as rapidly as possible.

At eight A.M. the iceboat was ready to start. The passengers climbed in and wrapped themselves in their travelling cloaks. The two great sails were hoisted and, under the pressure of the wind, the iceboat slid over the hardened snow. The speed increased more and more until the boat was skimming ahead at forty miles an hour.

The distance between Fort Kearney and Omaha, as the crow flies, was at the most two hundred miles. If the wind kept up, and no accident occurred, those miles might be covered in five hours.

The travellers, huddled close together could not speak for the cold. The icy wind lashed at their faces. Mudge crouched over the rudder, steering his craft, deftly avoiding rocks and obstacles that showed in their path. The prairie across which they were streaking stretched on and on like a great white sea. Since they had started, a strange singing had come from the metallic lashings that held the mast.

"Those chords give the fifth and the octave," said Mr. Fogg. They were the only words he uttered during the journey.

Aouda, cosily packed in furs and cloaks, was sheltered as much as possible from the attack of the freezing wind. She, too, remained quiet. Fix was so completely covered that only his eyes and the end of his nose showed.

As for Passepartout, his spirits had begun to lift as hope returned. If nothing went wrong, they would reach New York on the evening, if not the morning, of the 11th. There was still a chance to catch the steamer before it sailed for Liverpool.

Over fields and streams they streaked. At times, bands of ferocious prairie wolves ran howling after the iceboat. Passepartout got out his revolver and held himself ready to shoot any that came too near.

About noon they crossed the Platte River and were within twenty miles of Omaha. In less than an hour Mudge furled his sails. The iceboat, carried forward by the great impetus of the wind, sped on half a mile before it finally came to a stop.

Mudge pointed to a mass of roofs white with snow. "There's Omaha!" he shouted.

Passepartout and Fix jumped out and aided Mr. Fogg and Aouda to descend from the iceboat. The staunch owner, Mudge, was handsomely rewarded by Phileas Fogg. Then the party hastened toward the Omaha railway station.

A train for Chicago was ready to leave. They had just enough time to purchase tickets and swing aboard as the train got underway.

Excitement was building up like a fever in Passepartout. Every minute counted now if the steamer for Liverpool was to be caught.

The train passed rapidly through the state of Iowa. During the night it crossed the Mississippi at Davenport. The next afternoon, December 10th, they reached Chicago.

A connecting train for New York was waiting and the travellers ran to it. Nine hundred miles separated Chicago from New York.

Passepartout found himself leaning forward, as if willing the New York train to greater speed. And the locomotive seemed to respond.

It rushed through Indiana, Ohio, Pennsylvania, and New Jersey. At last the Hudson came into view. And at a quarter-past eleven on the evening of December 11th, the train stopped in the station on the right bank of the river, before the very pier of the Cunard Line.

But the mad dash had been all in vain. The steamship *China*, bound for Liverpool, had sailed three-quarters of an hour before.

Mutiny on the High Seas

AOUDA covered her face with her hands and sobbed. Tears were also in Passepartout's eyes. His master's last hope was gone. Even Fix looked as if he had lost his only friend.

But Mr. Fogg appeared completely unmoved. He calmly consulted his guide book for information on the departure of other trans-Atlantic steamers. The fast French vessel, the *Pereire*, did not leave until the 14th. All other steamers had later sailing dates or were not scheduled to touch at Liverpool.

"One to suit our purpose shall be found," said Phileas Fogg serenely.

The party spent the night at the St. Nicholas Hotel on Broadway. It was a wretched night for Passepartout, who tossed and turned and never closed his eyes. Mr. Fogg apparently slept soundly and was up early. He left the hotel alone, giving instructions for the others to hold themselves ready to depart on a moment's notice.

At fifteen minutes before nine, Phileas Fogg was back. He had come upon a vessel, the *Henrietta*, anchored off the Battery. She was departing in a matter of minutes for Bordeaux, France. Mr. Fogg had induced the owner and captain, Andrew Speedy, to take them along for the princely sum of two thousand dollars apiece.

As Mr. Fogg and his party departed for the *Henrietta*, Passepartout said, "But, Monsieur Fogg, we need to go to Liverpool, not Bordeaux."

"That is correct," said Phileas Fogg. "But the master of the *Henrietta* is a rather obstinate person and refuses to transport us to Liverpool. He will take us only to Bordeaux. However, such matters can be adjusted."

By nine o'clock, the travellers were aboard the *Henrietta* and a few minutes later she was moving across New York harbour. The last leg of the world voyage had begun.

At noon the next day, a man mounted the bridge to check the vessel's position. But instead of being Captain Speedy, it was, in fact, Phileas Fogg, Esquire. Unable to make Andrew Speedy change his mind about heading directly for Liverpool, Mr. Fogg, after shrewdly distributing money to the crew, had taken over command of the vessel. The unhappy Captain Speedy had been shut up in his cabin under lock and key.

Passepartout was thrilled by his master's magnificent manoeuvre. Now if the sea did not become too boisterous, if the wind did not veer around to the east, if no accident happened to the ship or its machinery, the *Henrietta* might cross the three thousand miles from New York to Liverpool in nine days and get there by December 21st.

During the first part of the trip, everything went smoothly. Mr. Fogg managed the *Henrietta* like a skilled seaman. On the 13th, they passed the edge of the Banks of Newfoundland, a dangerous area. There were frequent heavy gales and the sea was rough. Mr. Fogg gave orders to furl the sail and increase the steam. Fortunately, the bad weather did not continue.

December 16th was the seventy-fifth day since Phileas Fogg's departure from London. Passepartout was in good spirits. Half the voyage was over.

As for Captain Speedy, he continued to howl and growl in his cabin. Passepartout's duty was to carry him his meals, and the Frenchman was careful to use the greatest precautions when he entered the place.

Then, just as success loomed nearer and nearer, a disquieting note entered the picture. The engineer reported that he was running short of coal.

"We have kept up hot fires ever since we started, sir," he said to Mr. Fogg. "And though we had enough coal to go on short steam from New York to Bordeaux, we haven't enough to go at full steam from New York to Liverpool."

"Feed all the fires until the coal is exhausted," Phileas Fogg ordered crisply. "Our speed must be maintained."

The vessel continued to forge ahead at full steam until the 18th, when the engineer announced that the coal would give out in the course of that day.

Phileas Fogg called Passepartout and ordered Captain Speedy brought to him. Passepartout obeyed in fear and trembling.

It was like a bomb exploding when Captain Speedy landed on the poopdeck and confronted Phileas Fogg.

"You pirate!" raged he. "Where in blazes are we?"

"Seven hundred and seven miles from Liverpool," replied Mr. Fogg, calmly. "I have sent for you to ask you to sell your vessel!"

"Sell my vessel to a pirate? No!"

Mr. Fogg shrugged. "I shall be obliged to burn her. The upper part at least. The coal has given out."

"Burn the *Henrietta*," cried Captain Speedy. "A vessel worth fifty thousand dollars!"

"Here is sixty thousand," replied Phileas Fogg, handing the captain a roll of banknotes.

Captain Speedy's mouth dropped open as he felt the money in his hand. The *Henrietta* was twenty years old. Sixty thousand! It was a great bargain.

"And I shall still have the iron hull," said the captain in a softer tone.

"The iron hull and the engine. Is it agreed?"

"Agreed," said Captain Speedy.

Fix, the detective, who had listened to the conversation, seemed on the point of having a stroke. Another fortune in money gone. Soon there would not be any left.

Phileas Fogg quickly sent word to rip out the interior seats, the bunks, everything that would burn. Passepartout and the crew fell to with a will.

The next day, December 19th, the masts, rafts, and spars were burned. The crew worked lustily, keeping up the fires. Passepartout and Fix laboured with them.

The railings, fittings, the greater part of the deck and top sides disappeared on the 20th. The *Henrietta* was reduced to a flat hulk. But on that day, the Irish coast was sighted. By ten in the evening they were passing Queenstown.

Phileas Fogg had only twenty-four hours more in which to get to London. It would take that length of time for the *Henrietta* to make Liverpool under full steam. And with everything burnable consumed, the steam was about to give out altogether.

Mr. Fogg's decision was quickly made. They would enter the Irish port of Queenstown and take an express train to Dublin. There they would board one of the rapid boats that carried the mail across the Irish Sea between Dublin and Liverpool. By so doing, Liverpool could be reached by noon the next day, December 21, in time to make the run to London and arrive there by a quarter to nine in the evening.

This procedure was followed. At twenty minutes before twelve on the morning of December 21st, Phileas Fogg, accompanied by Aouda, Passepartout, and Fix, stepped ashore on the Liverpool dock.

Passepartout had a desire to throw up his hands and yell. Victory was practically in their grasp. A moment later, his excitement was abruptly extinguished.

He saw Fix draw himself up to his full height and stride importantly up to Mr. Fogg. The detective put out his hand and brought it down heavily on Mr. Fogg's shoulder.

"You are really Phileas Fogg?" he asked sternly.

"I am," said Mr. Fogg.

"I arrest you in the Queen's name!" cried Fix.

The Final Mistake

IT was past the noon hour, and Phileas Fogg was in prison. He was locked up in a room deep within the Customs House. The windows were heavily barred with iron rods. He was alone.

Outside the entrance to the Customs House stood Passepartout and Aouda, the picture of utter dejection, not talking, not even looking at each other.

When Passepartout had seen his master arrested, he had tried to throw himself at Fix and had only been restrained by policemen. Aouda had swayed and would have fallen in a dead faint if Mr. Fogg had not caught her.

"Do not despair," he had murmured. "All is not lost."

But to Passepartout, now separated from his master, no hope remained. Bitter thoughts assailed him. If he had only revealed Fix's true character and purpose to Mr. Fogg, all this might have been avoided. He had been the worst kind of fool.

Monsieur Fogg was now a ruined man. His fortune was gone. And he was facing trial as a bank robber.

Meanwhile, inside his prison room, Phileas Fogg was seated at a table. He had taken out his notebook and was in the process of making an entry: *21st December, Saturday, Liverpool. 80th day. 11.40 A.M.*

He heard the Customs House clock strike one o'clock and he glanced at his watch. He noted that his watch was two hours fast.

Two hours! If he were, at that very moment, taking an express train to London, he would be able to reach the Reform Club before nine P.M. The suspicion of a sigh escaped him.

At thirty-three minutes past two there came the sound of bolts being flung back. Phileas Fogg raised his head.

A moment later, the door was flung open and Passepartout, Aouda, and Fix rushed into the room.

Fix was out of breath. "Sir," he stammered, "I must ask you to forgive me. A mistake has been made. The bank robber was arrested three days ago. . . . He bore a most unfortunate resemblance to you. . . . You are free, sir."

Phileas Fogg rose to his feet, not quickly. With measured stride, he approached the detective. Then, with the only rapid motion he had ever made in his life, he drew back his right arm and with the precision of a machine knocked Fix flat on the floor.

"Well hit!" cried Passepartout.

Mr. Fogg turned toward the door. "Come along," he said to Passepartout and Aouda.

The three of them left the Customs House and took a cab. The railway station was gained in a few minutes. It was forty minutes past two. The express train for London had left thirty-five minutes before.

Phileas Fogg ordered a special train. There were several rapid locomotives on hand, but owing to the traffic on the line the special train was not permitted to leave until three o'clock.

The journey had to be made in five hours and a half if the wager was to be won. But there were forced delays, and when Mr. Fogg stepped from the train at the London terminus, the station clock showed ten minutes to nine.

He was already five minutes too late. He had lost his wager!

Phileas Fogg, his face expressionless as ever, walked from the station, closely followed by the heartbroken Aouda and the stunned Passepartout.

A carriage took all three to the house on Saville Row. Mr. Fogg said little as he entered his silent mansion. A room was set aside for Aouda, and Passepartout escorted the grief-stricken young woman to it.

The night passed.

The next morning Mr. Fogg called Passepartout and told him to get Aouda's breakfast and a cup of tea for himself. He informed the servant that he would be busy all day putting his affairs in order.

For the first time since he had lived in the house, Phileas Fogg did not set out for the Reform Club when the Westminster clock struck half-past eleven.

At half-past seven that evening, Mr. Fogg sent Passepartout to inquire if Aouda would receive him. In a few minutes Phileas Fogg found himself alone with the young woman.

"Madam," said he, as he seated himself near the fireplace, "when I decided to bring you to England, I was a rich man. I counted on putting a portion of my fortune at your disposal so that you could be free and happy. Now I am ruined."

Aouda's eyes filled with tears. "Mr. Fogg," said she, "you have saved me from death. You have been my protector. It matters nothing to me that you have no money." She hestitated, then went on, her voice low. "Mr. Fogg, will you have me for your wife?"

Phileas Fogg rose to his feet. There was a light in his eyes and he trembled slightly. He gazed full into Aouda's face.

"I love you," he said, simply. "Yes, I love you and I am entirely yours!"

"Ah!" cried Aouda, pressing his hand to her heart.

Passepartout was summoned and when he saw his master holding Aouda's hand in his own, the Frenchman knew what had happened. His round face became radiant with joy.

"If it is not too late," Phileas Fogg said, "kindly go to the Reverend Samuel Wilson, of Marylebone parish, and notify him that a marriage is to take place."

"Will it be for tomorrow, sir?" asked Passepartout. "For Monday?"

"For Monday," said Mr. Fogg.

Passepartout hurried off. It was then five minutes past eight.

In thirty minutes, the servant came rushing back into the room. He was so out of breath he could not, at first, speak.

"What is the matter?" asked Mr. Fogg, frowning slightly.

"My master . . . today isn't Sunday. It is Saturday!"

"Saturday? Impossible!"

"It is! It is!" cried Passepartout. "You have made a mistake of one day. We arrived twenty-four hours ahead of time. There are only ten minutes left to get to the Reform Club!"

Passepartout seized his master by the collar and dragged him toward the door. "Hurry! Hurry!"

And Mr. Fogg, propelled by his servant, moved rapidly for the second time in his life. He left the house running. He jumped into a passing cab. He yelled at the driver, promising him a hundred pounds if not a second should be lost in getting to the Reform Club.

The cab came to a stop in front of the club and Phileas Fogg stepped out. He paid the driver; then, resuming his methodical step, he entered the building.

Messrs. Stuart, Fallentin, Sullivan, Flanagan, and Ralph were assembled in the reading room. Each man had his eyes fixed on the wall clock.

As Mr. Fogg stepped across the threshold and entered the room, the hands of the clock indicated exactly a quarter to nine.

Phileas Fogg had accomplished the journey around the world in eighty days. He had won his wager of twenty thousand pounds.

And he had won a charming and beautiful young woman as a wife. For forty-eight hours later, Phileas Fogg and Aouda were wed. And it was Passepartout, glowing with pleasure, who had the honour of giving the bride away.

As the cab raced through the streets, Phileas Fogg worked out what had happened. Without realizing it, he had gained one day in his journey around the world because he had travelled constantly eastward He would have lost a day had he gone in the opposite direction Passepartout's watch, which had been kept to London time. would have shown this fact. if it had marked the days as well as the hours.